one hundred dollar misunderstanding

A Novel by Robert Gover

With a New Introduction by
Herbert Gold

A Grove Press Outrider Book
Grove Press, Inc. New York

AUTHOR'S NOTE

The caricatures in this story never were and aren't. If a reader happens to transmute them from typo-alphabetic symbols to figments of his imagination, they will continue to not exist, except as figments of his imagination. This also applies to the events which are this story—they didn't happen and don't. Any reader who imagines them happening is asked to please remember he is doing just that— imagining. In other words, the following story is a made-up, untrue story.

First Black Cat Edition 1980
First Printing 1980
ISBN: 0-394-17764-9
Grove Press ISBN: 0-8021-4332-6
Library of Congress Catalog Card Number: 80-19795

LIBRARY OF CONGRESS CATALOGING IN PUBLICATION DATA

Gover, Robert, 1929-
    One hundred dollar misunderstanding.

    First volume in a trilogy; the 2nd of which is Here goes Kitten; and the 3rd of which is J C saves.
    I. Title.
[PS3557.09205   1980]   813'.54   80-19795
ISBN 0-394-17764-9 (pbk.)

Manufactured in the United States of America

Distributed by Random House, Inc., New York

GROVE PRESS, INC., 196 West Houston Street,
New York, N.Y. 10014

INTRODUCTION

Innocence in a modern writer is always a paradox, and at this distance from the sixties, when *One Hundred Dollar Misunderstanding* came sporting into the world, Robert Gover's fantasy seems pure and loving. It had some of these romantic qualities even then, but the idea of a teenage black hooker and a square, Bermuda shorts college boy—this idea doing dirty things with itself—why, it was very shocking, very funny, very Grove Press. The book was also a Good Read, and surprisingly, with the additional element of the nostalgia we bring it, it is a more complicated Good Read now in the eighties. Kitten is worth exhuming though she would be a chuckly young grandmother by now. Even her love, surprisingly like the college boys of today, wanting to make out and do right, comes timely into the indirect low-current lighting of a besotted decade.

During a brief period when Black Humor was a phrase that seemed to mean something particular, I was appointed the reviewer of the somewhat-far-out for *The New York Times Book Review*. I did Henry Miller, Nelson Algren—not necessarily baby black humorists, you see—William Burroughs, Robert Gover, and a few others who seemed out of the mainstream but yet attention had to be paid. Interestingly enough, although fashion has passed

3

them all by, each holds up as an artist with an energy, tone, language, and rhythm of his own. And Gover, perhaps the most purely sportive of them, played games in this book which turn out to carry weight over the haul of a generation. Nostalgia may be a part of the charm; even Chubby Checker can still make the hips move a bit; but there is more than nostalgia here—a poignant little fable which casts the American paleface and the American goofberry against each other in a tender battle which remains a permanent part of our lives. Kitten is fun, and our college boy needs some. The boy has money, and Kitten needs some. Both need to climb out of the box trap life has set for them. Each may lose a leg in the escape, but, in the miracle of psychic wounding, they can grow new appendages. Such is the eternal power of love, a charm so bitter and caustic and juicy that it works even when it's not true, true, true-everlasting love.

And the money involved? What about the money? Well, that's a mere essential detail. Kitten lives by guile, and so does he. But they are both secretly ruled by love, or at least by unruly amorousness and lust. Kitten thinks she is making use of it and he knows he is being used by it. He tries to take a merely financial revenge...so goes the intrigue. Money sticks greasily to their hair. It'll wash away by and by.

"Think about grammar and a nightingale," Gertrude Stein said. The money over which Kitten and the Boy—now what the devil is his name?—quarrel is merely the grammar of their quarrel. The rest of the story, the fun, the haranguing combat, the concupisence, the erotic mystery contained within stuffiness, the yearning for an okay life contained within dishevelment and abandon, the force that through the flower drives the green fuse, the fuse that drives the flower through the green force, the need, the pleasant need of each of them for each other, a need made poignant by Kitten's equally imperative non-need, all these nightingales tumbled together chirp and peep resolutely, open their throats to sing in the dawn. *One Hundred Dollar Misunderstanding* is still young, green, and a nightingale — so what if a severe ornithologist, hiding in the grass, might notice that the full-throated warbler is only a mockingbird?

Kitten avoids self-pity by screeching. The Boy avoids it by not exactly avoiding it. Gover deals with his own self-regard by finding a headlong style and letting it take him to play.

We all know from simple observations, or passing our hands through it, that water could not support a body. Yet when we relax sufficiently in it, we can float, we can swim. So love cannot solve anything for us, and yet when we are splashing about on a fine day, it seems to justify everything.

Stories are about this paradox: Love is final, death will never occur; love is absurd, death is the ultimate consolation. Water will and won't support us. Gover grasps the problem rather fabulistically, as a joke. Not a bad way to go. He adds money, race, culture, language, all the elements which give reality to desire. That makes the pathos and the joke even better.

In this book Gover teases with an essential truth of poetry: We can never heap enough insult upon the unruliness of the heart. Nor enough praise. Out of the paradox comes tragedy or, in the case of understanding, a most affable farce. Penicillin and rue may be their destiny, but in the meantime there is blessed riot and misunderstanding. Despite everything, Kitten and what's-his-name are something like lovers in a closed place where love is not possible.

Their words fly out of the air, but their needs fly from more intimate places. The lissome lovely teenage hooker, black and swift, finds her chief need to be cash; money is not a symbol to her, it is a real thing for which she has a real lust, even if she won't spend it on what seems sensible to someone more grownup and less black. The chunky college lad, not overly swift in the head, definitely white bread all the way through, finds his chief need between his legs; he looks down at the querelous thing and it points upward to heaven and to Kitten. This is not symbol, either, or at least the reader doesn't feel it as such. It really seeks the old rub of meaning. It yearns, and it teaches the boy to yearn. The lovers may even go so far as to end up kissing and murmuring to each other.

Now I remember his name: College Joe.

And now the story begins.

—Herbert Gold

Immediately, right off the bat, without further ado, here and now, I wish to say that much of what happened to me that fateful week-end is completely unprintable, since it happened with a lady (colored) of ill repute. So all pornography-seekers are warned to seek elsewhere. I wish to make that point quite clear before proceeding further.

(Especially since Dad is chairman of our town's obscenity board so is well acquainted with the general subject and has impressed upon me the immense harm obscenity might do this great nation.) (Not 'that I'm a prude. Far from it! But nor am I a conveyer of illicit images and user of four-letter words and the mails to defraud.)

I mean, I plan to keep the telling of these unlikely events on as high a literary *plain* as I'm able, fully aware of my own shortcomings as I attempt this. After all, I'm a college sophomore, not a paid professional writer. You may ask why I didn't tell my experience to a paid professional ghost writer and have him write it for me. Well, I have a very good reason for that. I mean, for why I didn't do that. You see, I wish to remain anonymous for reasons which may or may not become clear to the reader, but are indeed clear to me. Only my legal initials will be used, but lots of others go by the same initials, so you'll never track me down from them.

So, to begin at the beginning, as they say, let me say that. . . .

Well, first of all, on Friday, we got our midterm grades and I found I was flunking three—repeat three —subjects (biology, psychology, French) and so the second half of that semester was going to be heck, sheer heck.

Second, Barbara, who is my steady girl friend, tele-phoned to tell me she received a telegram telling her to come home immediately, that her grandmother had died. Which proved coincidental.

You see, I also received a letter from my grand-mother and found in it a check for $100—a little birthday present. A bit late, yes, but better late than never, as they say.

Third, Dad called to say he was unable to bring me the Chevy for the weekend as per our previous agree-ment, that he had been urged by the hospital adminis-tration to attend some convention or clinic or some-thing in Cleveland or some god-forsaken place like that, and Mom needed the stationwagon, having planned for months to attend her annual bridge tournament in Boston, and that left the Caddy, which is only used for special occasions and which I couldn't get home to get anyway.

No car, no girl, and that second half semester star-ing me in the face! I was in poor condition, I can tell you. I mean, I was depressed—psychologically depressed!

You see—I've completely neglected to mention—it was the weekend of the big frat formal. It was *the* weekend of all weekends. And this year, Christmas! The formal was scheduled to be held at the Sheldon Country Club, no less—the swankiest place in town.

Some of the brothers tried to cheer me up by saying they could fix me up with a blind date, some freshman, and I could travel with my roommate, Hank, in his car, certainly. But . . . I was feeling just too too low. I mean! A man can weather a little ill fortune once in a while, but a triple whammy like that was too psychologically depressing. I was in *no mood*!

I mean, it was that psychological depression—that was the trouble. That's what led to all my difficulties. That and all the stuff I'd been hearing.

The thing is, I didn't have to flunk those subjects. I mean I'm not a stupe, by a long shot. As for the other two strokes of misfortune . . . Well, I was entirely a victim of circumstances.

Anyway, about nine o'clock that evening I found myself sitting there in that fraternity house completely by myself. Everyone else was either at the big dance or had gone home. There I was, in front of the TV in the livingroom, all alone. And that started me thinking, being alone.

It was probably Hank, who is always trying to fill my head with lewd thoughts, beating and beating his filthy obscenities into my mind. (I never asked to have him for a roommate. I barely knew him before I moved in. They just assigned me to a room and there he was.) He's constanly running off with a bunch of the brothers to some Negro house of ill repute, saying—and I repeat this one bit of smut only to show what sort of fellows I've been forced to live with— they're going to get their *ashes hauled*! That's a way of saying they're going to pay and then make love (or, I should say, fornicate) with some Negro. They think that little phrase they use is pretty funny. One night they sat around for over an hour and talked about nothing but. That phrase, I mean. One brother (he's a jerk) said he thought it was a sort of poetry. (Good grief!)

What I'm trying to say is I'm constantly subjected to this kind of talk. It's constantly being beaten and beaten into my ears. And Hank (who calls me Soph O'More, and thinks he's being funny because—so *he* says—sophomore once meant Wise Fool) (but he's never proven that statement with hard cold facts) —Hank is forever telling me I should go and have my ashes hauled.

Well, after making a great and sustained effort to respond as little as possible to that foul suggestion, I gave up and told him why I thought I shouldn't.

There are two very good reasons, too. Why I shouldn't, I mean. One, as I've already mentioned, is that Dad is a member of our town's obscenity board. Chairman, no less. And if word ever got back to him that I'd done, or even contemplated doing such a thing, well . . . I'm not sure exactly what would happen, but I am sure it wouldn't be good.

The other reason is that—contrary to what some of these brothers around here think—I'm no prude and have myself a couple of very good *un*professional ladies of ill repute (though that isn't really what they're called, ha ha) back home.

But when I finally did get around to telling Hank about them, he countered by laughing and saying I'd never be a man until— Well, I won't say it the way he did. What he meant was that I must miscegenate before I can consider myself much of anything. Which I know is entirely fantastic, a horrid idea and utterly ridiculous, unfounded on hard cold fact, unsubstantiated—an old wives' tale, for gosh sakes! No, I don't mean *wives* exactly. I mean it's just another obscenity like ashes hauled. And I, of course, realize this full well. As for my masculinity, I pointed out to Hank that my chest is very hairy and his hasn't a hair on it—not one! He tried to defend against this concrete evidence by laughing his same old deluded laugh, and also by sticking to his silly miscegenation as a criterion.

So please, Dear Reader, get this picture: Here I am sitting in front of this TV all alone in that empty frat house, left without a date, without a car, flunking at midterms three subjects—biology, psychology, French—stranded miles from home in this god-forsaken town with nothing but a little extra cash, feeling extremely psychologically depressed. I mean, this picture is important!

That and what Hank is always saying. I mean, he also talks as if the Negro is sexually superior to the Whiteman, for gosh sakes! *Then,* he tries to say *that* isn't what he *means*! I mean, when I point this out —when I tell him that, in effect, is what he is trying to tell me—he *denies* it. I keep trying to tell him how cockeyed his idea is, but he keeps insisting *superior* isn't what he means, and I keep trying to tell him superior is exactly the false conception he has, and he keeps trying to deny this, so I never do get my point across.

And to top things off, Hank, for gosh sakes, has amply demonstrated—though he won't admit this either—the extreme psychotic degree of confusion to which he and other brothers have gone by once saying that we live—and I now quote directly—in a state of whoredom—unquote. This, I was quick to mention, was an attempt to temper by rationalization the fact that he enters frequently into the sort of commerce transacted in non-white houses of ill repute.

But—like Max Shulman in those clever cigarette advertisements—I digress.

About nine o'clock, I thought: James Cartwright Holland, Holy Christmas! (An assumed name, as I mentioned earlier, though J. C. are, as a matter of hard cold fact, my initials.) (Sometimes I take an awful ribbing because of those two actual initials, as any quick-witted reader might readily guess, but I assure you they're actually legally mine.) I thought: Aren't things bad enough without sitting around thinking about them?

Then all the stories I'd been subjected to about this Negro house of ill repute (located in this red-light district with other houses, some of which have white girls, for crying out loud!) all these stories got the best of me and I decided to take a look for myself.

I mean, I certainly never intended to go fornicate with some paid professional woman of either race, I just meant to take a look for myself. I thought: When I return, I'll have an even clearer idea of what I'm talking about, so that next time I find myself in a discussion with Hank, I'll be even better prepared.

(As it actually turned out, my knowledge certainly was intensely deepened.)

So I checked my wallet ($135 in all) and took off for a night on the town. What I had in mind was going to this one bar the brothers are always going to when they have nothing better to do, where they have this jazz combo everyone says is very good, and where they also have paid professional ladies of ill repute floating about, sort of, because it's right smack dab in the middle of this redlight district. So I did. I went there. I took a taxi and went.

This place—it's called the Black-n-Tan—was, well, I don't know how to describe it. I wish I was (were) a writer so I could do it justice. (I mean a paid professional writer, of course, ha ha.) To begin with, it was jam-packed. It took me half an hour to work my way to the bar and then I got lucky and jumped onto a stool the moment some fellow left it. There seemed to be a lot of students in that place, but I didn't see anyone I recognized, so after awhile I relaxed and inspected the place. I just sat and listened and looked around.

I don't know much about jazz. I'll admit it—I don't. All I could tell was that one minute it was very loud and the next it wasn't. And it wasn't the sort of jazz you hear played on the radio. Also, the musicians (colored) seemed completely lost in what they were playing, and I could see where they would be. I couldn't tell where what ended and what began. The only thing I could conclude was that this type of jazz just wasn't *normal*.

But the people in that place! Wow! I'd never seen such a motley collection of people. In one place at one time, I mean. There was black and white and every shade in between. I even saw two Chinese students and a Chinese girl. And Christmas! At one end of the bar sat these two dolls—and I mean *dolls* —who were non-white, but pretty nevertheless. One had blonde hair, for gosh sakes! No doubt she dyed it, of course. And there was this guy with these two girls (you could tell he was with them by the way he would lean over and talk to them) this big, very-Negro guy dressed in an Ivy League suit and sitting there looking around as if he were looking for someone, expecting to see someone he knew. As a matter of fact, our eyes happened to meet once, while I was giving those girls the once-over, and he stared me down. Not only that, but the next time I looked up, there he was staring at me again. Christmas! He gave me the creeps! I don't mean he gave me dirty looks; I mean he kept looking as if we'd met some place and he suddenly recognized me. *Me*, for gosh sakes!

I was forced to conclude the two colored girls were paid professionals and he was sort of their solicitor, so to speak. (I'm aware that there's another word for what he was, but I'm trying to keep this factual narrative on a high plain.)

Though it's difficult, because the very next thing I knew, I was being tapped on the shoulder and when I turned around, here was some beady-eyed character (colored) staring at me. He said (and you may not believe this, but he actually said it): 'Looking for a date?'

'Certainly not!' I quickly responded. (To tell the

truth, I wasn't sure, at that moment, what he meant exactly, and was tempted to give him a taste of my knuckles, just in case.)

Then he said, 'Got some fine girls, right around the corner.'

Which clarified things. Somewhat.

But I said, 'No. No thank you.'

He said, 'Just looking around?'

And I said, 'Well . . . yes. As a matter of fact, I am just looking around.' Which, of course, was true.

'Okay,' he said, and moved on. He sort of shoved his way through the crowd along behind the stools. I watched him for a time, thinking: Well, James Cartwright Holland, you've seen yourself a real one for sure. It's official. (And I won't say what! But I became certain of my observations when he stopped a few stools from mine and tapped another fellow who looked like a university student.)

Well, that's the way it works. Enough said.

I went back to looking and listening, and hadn't been doing this long before the beady-eyed character returned. This time, all he did was tap and when I swung around, stared at me with this comical grin on his face. I thought: Well, after all, no one here knows me and I have yet to see the inside of a house of ill repute. What the heck! Question: Who would be the wiser? Answer: Me!

So I said, 'Where are your girls?'

And he started mumbling directions, which I didn't catch until I had him repeat them. I was to go out, turn left, walk to the corner and turn right, and the place was three doors down on the right.

The whole thing seemed just too fantastic. I mean,

I know such things go on elsewhere. But America! I'd always thought America was such a decent country. But then, even in the most decent country, the danger of moral cancer, as Dad calls it, is ever present. And don't get me wrong. I was not, for gosh sakes, diseased! I was curious. I mean, I owed this little excursion to my education, so to speak.

So, feeling very much like Dad must feel when he has to inspect things or places for indecency, I went. I mean, I felt like a detective. That's how I felt. I just adopted a very scientifically objective viewpoint on the entire matter and went. And my feeling of detecting increased handsomely when I discovered I was hot on the heels of two other university students.

But wow! What a neighborhood! I mean, I found myself deep in the heart of a slum area with inadequate housing and all that. I mean, they show pictures on TV of blighted areas and tell how they need more money for slum clearance and urban renewal, but gosh! They can't give you the sounds and smells on TV.

I'll try. (After adding that I walked slowly—past some pretty ugly-looking Negro men, just standing around doing nothing—walked slowly to let those other two students get ahead of me.) Right off the bat, as soon as I turned off the avenue onto the sidestreet —Bamb!

No lights!

In fact, there was only one streetlight the whole length of that block, for crying out loud! It shone down over a vacant lot right across the street from where I stood (on the corner).

Well, I was about to go back and catch a taxi and

take off for the frat house again, when I saw a sudden ray of light, and then those two college guys going in through a doorway—from which came the light, of course. Then I thought : Come come, JC, you're not going to be frightened off by darkness, for gosh sakes! Are you?

And right about here, I almost had a heart attack! There, right in the middle of that vacant lot, was this figure of a man. It would lean down and stand up and walk a step or two, then lean down again. I hadn't noticed him before, but there he was, all right. A rag picker, or something like that. Certainly a person of which to be leery. And, I can tell you, that, in spite of my scientific viewpoint, I was just that —leery.

So leery, in fact, that I began to worry about which door was the correct one to the ill repute house. I thought : Christmas, JC! Suppose you knock on the wrong door. Good gosh, in this neighborhood, no telling what might happen!

But I recovered from the sight of that dark and dismal figure of a bum picking about in that vacant lot (the police should have been notified, I realize), and went bravely forward. I thought : JC my friend you'll see the inside of an ill repute house if it's the last thing you ever do. And since you've come this far, you might as well keep up your courage and go on.

I did. Listening, all the time I was going bravely onward, to the most eerie-sounding barking dogs I'd ever heard. I mean, dogs barking here, there, everywhere. Not right where I was, exactly. But not so far away either. I couldn't be sure exactly where, I mean.

And, also, as referred to above, there were smells. Smells which you don't even get on TV public service programs. And a good thing, too, because they weren't very pleasant smells. It smelled dank, sort of. Like a mixture of wet earth and rotting lumber. It made me shudder, I can tell you. The whole place—that entire neighborhood made me shudder.

Still, I continued forging ahead. I marched. I said to myself, *Hup* two three four, *Hup* two three four, and marched! So that I finally made it to the third door from the corner, walked (marched) up the rotting wooden steps, and—Bamb!

Here goes me, I'm in the big chair. In come this trick by hisseff. College Joe. I kin tell them anywhere.

She-it! This one walk like he ain got no toes. Jittery? Kee-ryess is he jittery.

Jackie an Carmie upstairs wiff two tricks jes come in a minit fore this one. On'y hiyellas leff is Flow an Francine, so I spect this mothah gonna go up wiff Flow.

That godam Francine been botherin me agen, sittin on the arm o' the big chair an messin roun.

Madam tell this jittery Whiteboy we is all the cats they is jes now, an everybody waitin fer him t'pick one o'us. But he jes standin there, lookin roun the sittin room like he think more girls gonna come outta the walls.

I say t'myseff, Girl you gotta git yer Friday night cherry broke sometime, might jes's well try an hussle this jittery Joe. So I smile.

He lookin roun dum, my smile catch his eye an he smile back. Jes a lil ol bashful smile, like he fraid it gonna break his face, he smile fer real.

I smile agen an try lookin Pickaninny pritty, an he smile agen.

Madam see him smilin, she jes touch him on the back an send him on his way.

Nex, Gee-zuz! Francine stan up. She think alla time this daddio been smilin at her. She think he's fixin t'go up wiff her. Yeah! He so gee-gee jittery an all, she guess she gonna git his gun wiffout hardly no work. She likes them jittery tricks cause they pop fast, give her a chance t'jackoff an piss roun while us other cats go on workin.

But I stan up too. Yeah! An he nod t'me.

I say, Come on, pritty baby, we go upstairs.

He comin. He okay. Dress like he got loot. I say t'myseff, Girl maybe this trick like you enuff t'give you a pers'nal tip. Yeah! He dress like he got the jack fer tippin.

I say, This way, prittyboy.

Fore I swing on up, I look back at Francine an she lookin mean. Piss on Francine! I say t'myseff, I say, Keep a pucker' pussy, Francine, you'll get yer ass up-stairs okay. Don' worry, Friday's big night, lotta biz-ness fer everybody, Friday night.

She-it! That Francine, she ack like she wanna go wiff my trick jes cause he wanna go wiff me. How come she alla time buggin me?

Piss on Francine!

I swing ass upstairs an my trick come on along behind. Some College Joes grab ass when I swings it, but this mothah, he too jittery for grabbin. Bout all he kin do t'git up them stairs.

I take him on in this room Francine alla time callin her room. Yeah! Godam that Francine! Nobody give one fas' toot bout no room but her, an she gotta go callin this one room her room, counta the bed don' make's much noise.

I take me my jittery trick on the hell in that room anyhow! Yeah! Way that Francine ack, she ain gonna need her no room a-tall!

Them quiet jittery ones, they's trouble sometime. This mothah, I git him in that room, he jes stan there lookin dum.

I say, Well Hello, Sweet Baby. Wha's on yer mind?

He don' say nothin.

I say, Hey Lover, what're we gonna do?

An he jes look dum.

I say, Yoo-hoo, pritty baby, you wanna lil french? Haff an haff? How bout jes a straight? I say, Twenty berries an you alla roun the mothahfuggin worl'.

An then he look at me like he is gonna pee his pants! Right now! Yeah! I say, Mothahfuggin worl', an he bout t'shout.

Madam alla time tellin us cats, Don' never say *mothahfug* roun them real fay tricks, but Kee-ryees! Least that git him woke up some. Fore, he jes standin there lookin alla roun, dreamin. Jes dum an dreamy.

I say, Hey Baby, this a cathouse, you dig? This an no place t'do yer daydreamin at. I say, Cathouse fer funnin, Sweetheart. Yeah! How bout we do us some funnin?

An he still jes look dum. Gee-zuz! I don' know jes where the fug he think he is at. I can' be takin no all night fer one fast fiver, so I start in playin roun wiff his lil ol pecker. I'm playin, he's lookin roun real gone, an we jes gittin along like seven crabs in one big bumhole.

Nex, he look like he bout t'come alive, an he go t'say somethin, then he shut up agen.

Kee-ryess! Maybe he walk in here by mistake. What a muddlehead.

I start in all over agen. I say, Hey Baby, you feel like havin some fun?

He say, Yeah!

I say t'myseff, Well kiss my blackass! This mothah kin talk affer all!

Then I gotta tell him how much is what. Fack, I gotta tell him an tell him, an still he look dum. Yeah! I talkin, he standin there wiff a lil ol hardon, lookin roun real dum. Gee-zuz! How dum kin one Whiteboy git?

I say, Kee-ryess Sugar! I can' make it no plainer! Ain you got no jack?

He say, Huh?

I say, Ain you got no green? No loot?

He say, Huh?

I say, Ain you got no skins, no kale? No bread? No bones, no berries, no boys?

He say, Whaaa?

I say, Man yer in a cathouse. You come here, us cats figure you wanna do some screwin. Fore you do yer screwin, you gotta pay.

An kiss my lil ol blackass Pickaninny me, I say *that,* this daddio pull out the biggest fuggin wad o'green I ever in my everlovin born days ever-ever did see in this mothahless cathouse! Yeah! Ooh-ooh-ooh Skinny Minnie! That bundle cork my ass! Yeah! It knock me clean off my feet! He so fishfry flush he kin hardly git his mothahhumpin hands roun that wad! This baby lo-o-o-o-*did*! Ooh-wee!

I sit ass right down. I say t'myseff, Girl you jes let this sweet Whiteboy make up his own muddlehead what he wanna do. I say, Girl you jes be nice's ever you been. He got him enuff t'git him all the pussy he kin ever use!

Maybe I oughtta tell him, Hold the phone, man, I knock off work, we do the town! Like, on that wad, we kin dam well flyfug our way from here t'the moon an back. Yeah!

Sep, he jes standin there wiff his fay face all wrinkle up like a gran-mothah twoit, and he jes a-fingerin that everlovin stuff so nice, *so* nice! Way he finger, I know, I jes dee-diddly-dam well *know* him an it ain strangers.

Ain no wonner he's dum. All that mazoola, he kin be jes's dum's dum kin be!

Nex, this whole fuggin worl' start goin backwar's. Yeah! This trick, he standin there messin roun wiff his green, he say, What *you* wanna do?

Yeah! He say that! He ask *me* what *I* wanna do.

I bout pee! Kee-ryess! I dam well near tell him, I dam near say, Sweet Lovin Baby Sugar Doll, what I wanna do, I wanna fly! I wanna blow this cathouse an fly! I wanna bring you home t'Momma. I wanna hide you unner my bed!

But I don' say nothin. I git so diddly dizzy lookin that wad in the eye, all I kin do is sit an look.

He say, What you think best? He say, Wha's that you say bout roun the wor'? He say, Wha's this roun the worl', anyhow?

Meantime, I been gittin all fuss up over his wad,

I sayin t'myseff, I sayin, Girl you got you some fast considerin t'do. Yeah! This College Joe, he is loaded and he is jittery.

Jackie alla time sayin, Girl one o'these days yer gonna bump int'some nice invessment.

Look like I bump! Now what the hell m'I gonna do?

Jackie say, Treat invessment real real fine, an he ask you yer phone, an then yer in bizness. Yeah!

On'y I know what *he* wanna do, I kin treat him real fine, but he ain sayin. He askin me what *I* wanna do. Kee-ryess! An then he askin bout roun the worl' an alla time so jimjam jittery he ain gonna make it t'the corner!

She-it!

Nex, I say, Baby you don' want you no roun the worl'. Right now, jes yet. What you wanna do, you wanna stay fer the whole mothah—Eh, you wanna stay fer all night!

He say, No. He say, He don' wanna do that. He say, He don' like the looks o'this place.

What the fug the looks o'the place got t'do wiff it? Ooh-wee! I do me some more considerin.

Then I say, Tell you what, Sugar. How bout a lil ol haff an haff, jes fer now, like. See how you like that. Huh?

He say, I say so, tha's okay by him.

Gee-zuz!

I say, Okay man, *I* say so.

He say, Fine.

Bless my blackass Pickaninny me!

Nex, he say, How much?

Ooh-ooh-ooh Skinny Minnie! Might je's well git me a lil ol English tip right now!

I say, Ten.

He say, Ten dollah?

What the fug he think? Ten peenuts?

I say, Yeah man, ten dollah.

Counta my considerin tell me, invessment or no invessment, this sweet baby got so much I might jes's well git me three lil boys fer myseff.

See, haff and haff really on'y cost seven, but crap! He ain gonna miss him no three outta that wad. No-oh-oh! He give me a five and five ones. I'm gonna git me three. Yeah. Tha's English tip.

Sep, he go an give me a *spot*, I ain gonna git me no three. I gotta go an put three in the tipbox fer all them other cats t'share my three, he give me a spot. I don' mind sharin, but I kin always use me three o'my own. Yeah!

So Kee-ryess! He do. He give me a spot, an that finish that.

I ask him, Ain you got no lil bills, man?

He say, No. He say, Sorry.

So I don' git no English tip. I stick that ten tween my titties an swing ass down the hall. I pay up seven an git back three and put them three in the tipbox, an then I go fer the soap an water.

At first I thought my ears were deceiving me. Such language! From a girl! I mean! Even if she was non-white, such profanity! (I certainly won't repeat what she said, You'll just have to take my word for it that it was foul, dirty, and in exceptionally poor taste.)

And that room! I was flabbergasted! (I mean, this room this woman of ill repute took me to. A description of which will follow.)

Also, the downstairs! (Of the ill repute house.) (Which, I fear, I'm unable to describe without jeopardizing the high literary plain I'm attempting to maintain.)

And the stairway! It was practically as wide as a linen dispenser and every bit as steep as a ladder. (I'll bet that house was a hundred years old if it was a single day!) And this girl (yes, as you may have surmised by now, I permitted myself to continue along with this misadventure) (or investigation, as I prefer to think of it.) (After all, I thought: JC, it's now or never!)—this girl (I mean, this professional prostitute) wasn't as bad looking as I'd expected. She was Negro, yes, and she had that tight kinky hair and—well, she wasn't at all white in any way. I mean, there was a partly white one sitting on the arm of the chair in which sat this one which I picked out, but I figured as long as I was where I was when I was, I might as well pick a dark one. She wore a black blouse and a tight red skirt and didn't look very old. Matter of fact, she appeared approximately my age. (Nineteen.) But Christmas! Going up those narrow stairs, I almost bumped into her rear end, it was so dark. I mean, it wasn't so dark I couldn't *see* her rear end (which certainly did stick out far enough) (for such a little person, I mean) (in that tight skirt and all) (presenting me with two shiny spots, for gosh sakes!) but it was about all I could do to keep from bumping into her. It's a good thing we had only one flight up to climb. The way she swayed her rear end, I might have ended up hypnotized. (I mean, like you can become hypnotized watching a pendulum swinging back and forth.)

And the second floor was just one long hallway with doors all along either side, and one bare light-bulb hanging up for light. (Of course.) (But it didn't throw much, is what I mean.) Then, right off the bat, the next thing I knew, we were in this tiny little room and she was talking.

Which is where the big trouble really began. I mean, I couldn't understand a word she was saying. At first. Gradually, as I got acclimatized to her dialect, I began hearing the wildest, most unprintable obscenities I think I've ever heard—and I mean I've been around. Around women who swore, even, but not this way. Hence, Dear Reader, even though I quite possibly might, at this juncture, give a snatch or so of dialogue, the language she employed was so utterly indecent it would have to be thoroughly censored before it would be legally permissible. And I am strictly against censorship. Therefore, I refrain from direct quotations. I mean, even a writer of filth could never quote such a person verbatim and expect to get it past even the lower courts. Her entire vocabulary, such as it was, seemed composed of pornographic slang and insincere endearments.

But, finally, I got so I could understand her enough for us to conduct our business transaction, so to speak.

But that room threw me. I certainly wish I was a paid professional writer so I could describe it to you. I'll try.

There was a lightbulb. I mean, this one bare lightbulb, and that's all. And there was a bed. Or, almost a bed. Really, it was just an old bedframe with an old mattress on it and an old bedspread over the mattress. And when I say old, I mean old! And the walls—good gosh, the walls! The wallpaper looked like it held up the entire building. And you couldn't be certain how much longer the building was going to hold up! Because the wallpaper was just sort of . . . disintegrating. It was crumbling and peeling off and just coming off the walls right before your very eyes! Under the wallpaper there were strips of old broken wood, only. Flimsy? Wow! Then, beyond those strips —upon which the wallpaper was *supposed* to hang— there was nothing but a surface, very substandard, which I am forced to conclude was the inside of the outside of that clapboard building—if you can call it a building.

Anyway: this room. The excuse for a bed was

just inside the door to the right, between the door and the right wall. The room was that small. The left wall was that crumbling wallpaper and the right wall was sort of a partition affair—very temporary looking, but like it might hold up longer than the other wall. Because it was newer, I mean. The far wall (also disintegrating) had a round hole in it, which I was forced to conclude was supposed to serve as a window. And in the far right corner stood this dresser. Or, what had been a dresser. It no longer had drawers, just openings where drawers were supposed to be. And on top of it, looking very very out of place, sat this vase! With flowers in it! Imagine! Flowers in that room!

The floor was old wood and bare. Just as bare as anything. Nothing could be bare-er than that wooden floor.

And, believe it or not, that was all there was to this tiny room. I know that sounds fantastic, but it's factually true. Just this bed, the skeleton of a dresser, and that's all.

But the girl (did I neglect to describe her?) wasn't bad. I mean, of course, bad *looking*. For a nonwhite. I mean, she was, as they say, ha ha, stacked! Not at all what I'd expected. Though don't get me wrong. I'm not prejudiced. Far from it.) She had a very childish face. Also very dark. And eyes which were large and watery looking, with drooping eyelids, which never seemed to look directly at you. (Me.) And her voice was tiny and high-pitched, like a young girl's. Though, of course, I realize she had to be at least my age—at least—in order to be there.

But she moved like she was 60. That was the thing.

I mean, she moved slow and easy—very slow. (Coming up the stairs, she even swayed her rear end slow, unlike most girls whom I know of, who are white, of course, and wiggle—if they do—quickly and nervous like. Squirrelly, if you get what I mean.)

But I don't, for gosh sakes, wish to dwell unduly on physical detail. So I will skip recounting certain actions she went through, as well as certain phrases she used while going through these afore-mentioned actions.

And, until we got around to sealing the transaction (if you can call it that) she seemed utterly and completely detached. I mean! Talk about scientific detachment! Scientists should be so detached! As a matter of hard cold fact, it was her detachment which aggravated me. I don't know what I had expected, but I had not expected detachment, for gosh sakes!

Just one word about her lingo. Or, as much of it as I could catch. She muttered something about, among other things, French. Which made me think of my flunking grades—biology, psychology, French—and for one fraction of a second, I thought she wanted to discuss grades and other aspects of university life, though I certainly had no idea how we might go about such a discussion. She and I, I mean. However, this proved an erroneous assumption on my part. (As I learned later, French, in her dialect, meant something entirely different and as unprintable as nine-tenths of her jargon.)

She finally sort of fell back down on the bed and sat there looking slightly shaken, though for the life of me I was unable to learn what had troubled her. I didn't wish to appear boorish (I try to treat all

peoples as equals, regardless of race, color or creed)
so I asked, in an attempt to snap her out of her sudden
mysterious depression, how she would like to spend
our time together. (And I wish to make it quite clear
that—at this point, at least—I certainly had not resorted to any rationalizing or anything like that. But,
after all, I had never found myself in an ill repute
house before, and was not, for gosh sakes, familiar
with their customs.) (I mean, by asking, I wished to
kill two birds with one stone. I wished to disrupt her
detachment, engage her interest in me as a person, so
to speak, and also—second—to show her that I was
magnanimous enough to consider her feelings in the
matter, even if she was a paid professional of another
color.) And apparently I was successful in this double-
barreled endeavor, for she looked up after a moment
of depression with new interest. (No doubt such persons have their own brand of troubles.) And we com-
pleted our business. I mean, it turned out that one
pays in advance, so I paid.

I must add here that I did feel a bit uneasy carrying my money into that place at that time, because
of the sort of neighborhood I was in, and all that. I
mean, you never can tell. So many people lived in
that neck of the woods who don't seem to want to
go out in the world and get themselves a good job and
advance themselves—and that sort of attitude is communistic and breeds crime. But she paid absolutely
no attention to my money (which I carried bare in
my trouser pocket, having had the good sense to leave
my wallet back at the frat house in view of the type
of neighborhood I was entering.) (I mean, if somebody was going to rob me, they certainly wouldn't

get my valuable papers.) So I concluded she was too distracted by some sort of personal problem to be concerned with my money. And as it turned out, this was the first of a series of miscalculations on my part, which later led to a larger misunderstanding.

But, like those clever cigarette advertisements again, I digress.

Eventually, during our little preliminary conversation (or *un*conversation) she became more friendly and began sounding not honestly insincere. I mean, she seemed to drop her false sincerity when I demonstrated that I wished to be anything but boorish, and became, well—her entire approach toward me changed.

I thought : After all, JC, you do have something about you which attracts the ladies. And even if she is a paid professional lady of ill repute, she, after all, is human. Mom says it's that you're a natural born salesman. Why fight it?

Then, the next second, the very next thing I knew —Bamb !

Gone. She was gone out the door, leaving me in that dismal cell by myself. Didn't say a word about where she was going or when she'd get back, simply went !

Well, I don't mind admitting at this point that I was just a little shaken. I didn't know whether to go after her or wait patiently for whatever might happen next. But I kept my head and waited. (Which, it seems, is accepted procedure.) And as it turned out, what happened next was not on the menu.

Here goes me, I come back. He tells me this other cat been in. I say, Who?

He say, He don' know who. He say, Firs' time in any cathouse, how he sposed t'know who's who.

I dam near believe it's his firs' time in any cathouse. I bout ready t'believe he fresh off some lost boat someplace. I bout ready t'believe anythin this mothah wanna tell me.

He tell me this other cat wearin a blue dress. He say, *Cocktail* dress!

Yeah! He say that! Hee hee!

On'y one Jane in this cathouse got her a blue dress on, an tha's Francine. I tell him fergit it.

But I gotta laugh. Francine all cocktail set t'go up wiff this big fat ol wad o'jack. She think he wanna go wiff her. Alla time he pick my lil ol blackass Pickaninny me. Yeah! He my trick. He gonna like me. He gonna like me so much, he gonna ask me my phone!

Piss on Francine!

Nex—I been so all fuss up bout that sweat wad— I ain even seen he still dress'. He standin there wiff all them clothes on. How come he don't take 'em off so's when I git back we is all set?

She-it! This speed, he gonna be all night fer one lil ol haff an haff.

Jackie alla time sayin, Invessment is give an git, give an git.

But Madam alla time sayin, You cats git an git. Git yer ass upstairs and git them tricks off an git yer ass back downstairs. Don' be no mothahless whole night fer one dum five-bill College Joe. She say, They ain got no loot worff worryin bout.

Yeah! Madam say that!

Kee-ryees! I got news fer Madam.

Sep, fore she git her news, I gotta do right so's he ask me my phone, so's I kin git me my invessment. Oncet I git givin an gittin, an we goin along invessment-fine, then I kin tell Madam. First, fore I kin do nother blessed thing, I gotta College Joe undress' t'git.

I say, Sweet Baby, you ain undress'? How come?

He say, Huh?

Gee-zuz!

I say t'myseff, Girl he can' unnerstan what yer sayin, on'y one way t'do. Ack it out. So I do. I do this right unner the light so's he kin look me over real good. He look. He lookin real hard. Then I'm standin there waitin, an he is still lookin. He look dummer an dummer.

I say, Baby you wanna keep yer clothes on?

He say, No! He say, Course he don' wanna keep his clothes on.

Ooh-wee!

I say, Honey you don' wanna keep 'em on, thing t'do is take 'em off!

He say, Yeah sure yeah! An he start in.

An he got a long way t'go. Kee-ryess!

But I say t'myseff, I say. Hol' yer ass, Girl. This mothah kin be jes's dum's he wanna be, he got him that much mazoola.

He fold his clothes over the chair real careful. I ack like I'm daydreamin, he do that. He so dum, he might git t'thinkin I wanna rob him. He ack a wee bit mistrussful anyhow. He ack that way, I ack like I'm the dummes' lil Pickaninny livin.

I gotta long wait till he finish undressin, he got so much on.

I wash him real nice an soff, counta him bein so awful tickledingus, and then I gits t'work. Time I start in, I got me so many worryful considerins t'do, I can' hardly pay no mind t'teckneek. Workin an considerin, an wonnerin does this dum Whiteboy know what t'do wiff that thing fer the other haff o'his haff and haff, I find I done me too dam much considerin.

Nex, I ain been at him a minit, an pop, off he go!

Kee-ryees!

An then—I git up an go on over t'the basin—this Whiteboy, he sit up like a mothahjumpin jack-in-a-box an he start lookin at me like I done somethin wrong.

Gee-zuz! All that Jack an I can' make nothin go right, he so fuggin dum. Come in here all loaded up like that an I don' even git a chance t'show him how good I kin do. Naecher done mess me up at the most baddest time.

An he still lookin, Gee-zuz!

Then he say, That all?

Yeah! He say that! He say that like he think I sposed t'do a lil dance fer him nex. Kee-ryees!

I say, Yeah Baby, tha's all. Dam shame, too.

He say, Yeah it's a shame. He say, One ain never enuff fer *him*!

I feel like sayin, Baby way you go off, you musta been savin that *one* fer a mothahlumpin lifetime. On'y you ask me my phone, I fix you up fer the rest o'yer lifetime, long's you want. You ask me my phone, you ain never gonna go so long wiffout pussy you gits *that* trigger-happy agen.

But I don' say nothin and he don' ask me my phone. Can' blame him. I don' even git me a chance t'show my stuff. *Poof*! Invessment gone.

I start in t'git dress' agen, feelin real blue, an he jes still layin there lookin real surprise, like I ain doin right.

I say, Come on, Baby, we gotta git outta here.

He say, Le's go nother one.

I say, Can'. Ain allowed, man. You gotta—

An then I cork ass an start in considerin all over agen. Hell! He done pay ten fer haff and haff an don' even git him one haff. But Kee-ryees! We been up here so mothahfuggin long now, Madam gonna send for the firetruck, we don' git ass back downstairs. I say t'myseff, Gee-zuz Girl! You jes can' go breakin rules fer no trick too dum t'ask you yer phone an git him a lil o'yer ass on the side.

But I can' help tryin one more fishline. I say, Baby ain you got you no sweet lil chick fer that pritty cock?

An she-it! Seem like I jes can' say the right thing

roun this dum mothah. He wrinkle up an he start in tryin t'tell me he got him plenty.

I bout t'give him up fer lost. I say t'myseff, This daddio so dum, he gonna end up comin backwar's. Yeah, he gonna end up backfirin. He soun like he is backfirin right now.

Then he quit jawin that crap an he say, Come on, le's go jes one more real quick.

Real quick, he say. Hee hee! His lil ol genrill still up an lookin peppy. Madam say, trick wanna go agen, he pay up right now, else he start in from downstairs all over agen. But this poor mothah done pay fer haff and haff and don' even git haff, and I is out one big fat invessment chance. Gee-zuz! This ain right!

So I say, Now?

He say, Yeah now. Real quick, real quick.

Las' trick say that make me break the rule too, an he pay agen an then he turn out so fuggin slow on the secen', he dam near wear my ass clean out. Course, that weren't the same. That one, he don' give me no insprashun. This one, he the biggest invessment chance I ever seen in this cathouse. He dum, yeah! But crap, he can' help *that*!

I say t'myseff, I say, Ain no good leavin him go downstairs an pick him out some new cat an give her her chance t'make invessment when I got him up here wiff me right now.

Piss on Madam an her git and git!

I say, Baby you promise t'be real quick an don' never tell nobody I do it?

He say, Yeah yeah yeah!

I say, Sure you kin go agen so quick?

He say, Sure sure sure!

I tease a lil more. I say, An you ain gonna tell nobody?

He say, No no no, he ain gonna tell.

I say, But Sugar, I better not. I say, We been up here too long already. I say, Go on, git! Go git you nother girl.

He look real sad, I say that. He look like he gonna go an find him nother girl. Fer real!

Gee-zuz! Ain nothin gonna go right fer me t'night?

I say—real fast—I say, Whoa Baby! I laugh. I say, I'm on'y teasin.

An I outta my clothes agen an on that bed so fast he don' know which end is up. I say, Shove over, Lover. I say, Honeydripper, make room fer this Honeydripper!

He do.

Nex, he no sooner in the saddle an we is jes bout ready t'raise hell when—

Gee-zuz Kee-ryees! The godam Francine pop in. Yeah! Loud's a fart in a empty tincan.

She say, Kitten yer in *my* room.

I say, Francine godam yer crazy ass, git outta here!

I kin see my trick gittin all jittery all over agen.

Francine, she say, Don' you know by this time, this *my* room?

I kin feel his ol soljer jes a-wiltin an wiltin.

I say, Come on Baby, don' pay no nevermind t'her.

But he jes too fuss up. Counta Francine bein there.

I say, Francine up yers wiff a lawnmower, you git yer greezy hair the hell outta here.

An she say, Girl who you think yer talkin to?

An I say, You you cottinpickin crab nabber.

An she say, Don you talk t'me like that, you lil bitch, or I'll ruin you.

An I say, Francine can' you see I'm busy jes now? Now how come you don' git?

An she say, No. She say I gotta git, go find nother room.

I say, Francine yer flippin yer lid! You git right now or I'm gonna call fer Madam.

She say, like hell I'm gonna call fer Madam. She tell me *she* is gonna call fer Madam, I don' git. She say, I goin right downstairs right now an tell Madam yer in my room an yer takin all fuggin night for one lousy trick.

So I say, Okay Francine, go on, tell Madam.

She ain gonna tell Madam nothin. She do, Madam kick her ass right out! Francine, she don' belong in no cathouse nohow. She don' git along wiff nobody, hardly. She ack like hers don' stink. It do.

Time she git her crazy ass the hell outta there, my poor lil ol Joe College done wilt like somebody bust his balloon, an I gotta start in all the everlovin over agen. Kee-ryess!

I ain never been nobody fer fightin, but Gee-zuz! I fraid I was bigger, I'd lose my blackass Pickaninny head fer considerin an jes take an kick livin hell outta that Francine.

I gotta work real fast now. We was late fore she come in an we ain getting no sooner.

I start in playin nice's I kin unner the circumstances but I gotta start in from scratch. Kee-ryees! I'm talkin pritty's ever I kin, an playin nice's I know how, an he comin along okay.

An nex, Gee-zuz! I git me more trouble!

This muddlehead pull up an look down on me real sad—real real sad—an he start in talkin sad too. Steada hoppin back in the saddle on goin, he is gonna try some make believe sweet talkin. He start in ackin like he's playin him some dum movie scene. Yeah! He talk sad an then he look at me like I'm sposed t'talk sad back.

Ooh-wee! He lose me!

I don' know what t'do. I considerin that jack he got an I considerin how long we been up here an I hearin more tricks jes a-streamin in that mothahless front door downstairs, an I jes *know* Madam gonna wonner what the hell happen t'me.

I say, Sweetheart Lover, we ain got *time* fer that *now*! I say, You tol' me you gonna be quick. Here you go pissin roun like you think I got all fuggin night! I say, Gee-zuz Baby, Madam gonna think yer eatin my ass, steada—

Now godam, come on, Baby. Giddy up!

I say all that nice's I kin at that time, an I make him smile. He do that, I hope t'toot an back he git the idea t'ask me my phone, but he don' git that idea a-tall! No!

Nex thing I know—jes bout the time we startin t'go good an I gits movin okay an I goin fine's I ever do go, and I snappin the whip an punchin the apple, an I wonnerin is my invessment ever gonna come thru an ask me my phone—an I rollin ass eas' an rollin ass wes', an breakin my poor ol Pickaninny back fer this dum mothah—nex thing I know, he git him one more dee-diddly-dum idea, an fore I know what he is tryin t'do, he got my ass hung up clear off that bed!

Yeah!

I say, Hol' it, Baby! What the fug you doin?

She-it! I open my big mouff and that son-a-bitch jes stop, plop, an lay deadweight. Seem every cottin-pickin thing I do jes backfire. I git me nothin but trouble trouble trouble.

He say, He don' know wha's the matter. He say, Seem like *I* is doin all the *work*!

Yeah! He say *I* is doin the work!

I bout flip my lid right here. I say, Gee-zuz, Sweetie! An I try best I kin t'talk nice. I say, Course *I* is doin the work. What the hell you think? I say, *I* is the *cat*, *you* is the *trick*! Unnerstan? I say, Now come on, Lover, giddy up oncet agen an le's git the hell outta here. I keep tryin t'tell you, we ain got no *time* right *now*—fer talkin.

I say—an alla time tryin t'soun nice—I say, Giddy the sweet everlovin horsey ass up oncet agen, please!

Well she-it! He start in goin, yeah! Sep, this time he got him nother fancy fug idea, an he start in wham jammin me like he's choppin rock. Yeah! He jes a-gruntin an rammin away like he's mad at the whole mothahhumpin worl'.

Course, I know better'n t'open my big mouff *this* time. I keep tryin t'do my stuff best I kin unner the new circumstances, but it ain easy.

Meantime, I'm thinkin we jes gotta make it this time an he can' git him nohow no more new dum ideas—an he git him nother one. Yeah! He do!

Gee-zuz! I don' know how one dum Whiteboy kin behave so mean! This time, he curl my blackass right up double an he piledrive like he is tryin t'stan me on my poor ol Pickaninny head an bump me straight down t'hell!

Yeah! He do that! I don' know what he is tryin t'prove, but I ain bout t'ask no more queshuns.

On'y thing I try, I try a lil reverse English. I say, Tha's-a-way, Baby! Hit it, Sweetheart! Go go go!

He go! An he git him his dee-diddly-godam ten dollah gun. At las'!

I up outta that bed and doosh on the run an dress —right now! I even fergit all bout that invessment idea, I so scared my ass gonna be mud, time I git back downstairs.

I say, Hey Lover, how come you wanna ack like that? You think pussy made o'steel?

I laugh when I say that. It ain easy, but I do.

He laugh too, dum she-it.

Good thing I laugh.

Even though I am trying to keep this on a high literary plain, I feel it is obligatory at this point that I go into the matter of my past experience with women. For reasons which will become clear to the intelligent reader, I'm sure.

As I formerly mentioned, there are these two *un-*professional ladies of ill repute I happen to know at home. One is Marge and the other is Susie. Despite their already ruined reputations, I refuse to mention their last names. I'm not a cad, for gosh sakes! On the other hand, I'm not a prude either. What I mean to say is, I'm just a normal nineteen-year-old fellow, with normal appetites and all that, and these girls (at home) are always calling me up anyway. Don't get me wrong—I certainly don't go with either one of them. As previously mentioned, Barbara is my girl, and she's a very high-minded girl too. I wouldn't *touch* Barbara. I'm not that type. As a matter of fact, we may marry some day. But marriage, for me, and also for Barbara, is in the future, so as I've already mentioned, there are these two girls at home, whom

I occasionally date. I mean, *go out with*. I can't really consider them *dates,* for gosh sakes !

What I'm driving at is this : Both of them consider me the best lover in town. I don't mean to brag, but they do. They're constanly telling me they do, and they've been telling me this for some time now. And I'm fully aware that the reason they feel this way—even though they run with any number of other fellows, being the sort they are—is that I'm far from unendowed physically. Also, I know how to handle myself in the backseat of our family Chevy. Though, again I must emphasize, I'm not trying to brag. I'm only stating the facts, the hard cold facts. And as for my being loose enough to run with these two, I must mention that I do not wish to enter wedlock, especially with such a fine girl as Barbara, completely naive about such important matters as the techniques of love-making.

Enough said. About that aspect, I mean. I do not wish to dwell on such matters incessantly. I point the above out only to emphasize the sort of fellow I am.

And as a preliminary to a comment on my ill repute experience. Which is, namely : Much to my surprise, I found that in certain respects Hank was almost right. I mean, he doesn't really *know* it. He's half right without knowing it. He's right in that colored girls are not the same. That is, *this* colored girl I found myself with was not the same as either Marge or Susie. In several regards.

Not that I'm ready to concede to Hank's idea that Negro girls are somehow, in some mysterious way, *superior* (and I insist that, despite his denials, superior is what he means) to white girls. No, he's wrong about that, and I was forced to conclude I was even more right than I had realized.

But different—that's my point. For instance (and this will be difficult to tell without becoming obscene) this colored professional prostitute had the same inclination that Margie has, except she went about it . . . Well, she went about it *more* so than Margie ever did. I mean, she just acted as if it was quite natural, as I suppose, in view of her status, it was. Though I found her manner of approach more than slightly disquieting. I mean, it was so professional, so undramatic and lacking in the necessary preliminaries. It was startling, almost sickening, for gosh sakes!

I suppose, however, that never having been to a house of ill repute, I had acquired certain misconceptions about how such women behaved—based on my natural, normal experiences. Experiences unpaid for, is what I mean.

In fact, I was so surprised by her manner of approach (and also by a couple of unlikely intrusions by some other paid professional colored girl, who kept opening our door and sticking her head inside, first while mine was gone, and then later) that I reached my first (if you'll pardon the expression) climax a bit too hastily. (I should also add that the surroundings I found myself in had something to do with the above.)

I then learned that it's one climax per customer, for gosh sakes! One and you're out. Well, again I don't mean to brag, but when I go out with Margie or Susie, one is far from enough. For me, at any rate. So, when I learned I was considered finished by this colored girl after that one, I objected. She then told me that this was the rule and that I had to go.

But—unsatisfied with my unsatisfactory experience, and convinced that I had much to learn about this phase of life (paid prostitution) before I could consider myself really truly a man of the world, I turned on the old sales charm and convinced that professional she should break her rules, just this once. Which she did, making it more evident that she found me to her liking.

And, at this point, I might add that, having the sort of analytical mind I have, I'm prone to vary my intellectual approach from time to time, and at times I think in representations. In fact, I began thinking in representations when this girl first approached in the hitherto described manner. I thought : Poor thing ! Offspring of Southern slavery. And here she is (to my representation thinking) a slave once more. (I mean when she was going about it in the perverted way.) Here I am, the white master, just laying back while she works with no compensation—much like some nasty white slaveholder might have sat on his veranda, sipping mint julips, while a gang of slaves picked his cotton.

Then, that thinking was interrupted, and later, after I'd persuaded her to break that house rule, I returned to thinking in representations, and I thought : From slave to employee ! Now, at last, emancipation ! And she now works under me as part of an actively engaged company team—employer and employee. Compensation at last ! But is her compensation adequate ?

(And it is about right here that we were interrupted by this other prostitute, who stuck her head in through the door—a most perturbing habit she had. There seemed to be absolutely no privacy in that place. And she and my girl got into an argument about whose room it was we were in, and both of them shouted the most vile profanities at each other, until the other one left, and I went back to thinking) :

Is she adequately compensated? After all, she likes me, and after all, I'm here to find out, to learn about a phase of life I've never come into contact with. Why don't you, thought I, JC my friend, be a good employer and up her wages? (Representatively thinking, you understand.) Why don't you—One, show her you are far from a prejudiced white person, and Two, that you know how to handle yourself in bed with a woman, no matter what the color of her skin.

What I mean is, even though she was (to my representative thinking) at that time my employee, she was doing all the work. I thought : Good gracious, JC, this will never do. You, after all, are the one who should carry the old football, so to speak. You are the male component.

So I did. I mean, I went about showing her that I could, after all, handle myself with a woman. I thought : It's about time she found out that even though she's the employee (representatively thinking) I'll let her know I'm every bit as good at this sort of business as she is, and by letting her know, I'll increase her wages and decrease her working effort, causing a marked rise in plant efficiency.

I mean, ha ha, just a manner of thinking—in representations.

But, lo and behold, I had apparently broken some other house rule, for I learned she had not expected me to take the initiative in our—well, you know what I mean.

But, having broken one house rule to reach this stage, I decided to ignore that second house rule as well, and to proceed as per my original representation thinking, which I did. I let her have it. I mean, I showed manly initiative—the way I do especially with Susie—and showed that ill repute colored girl a thing or two. I mean, I let her know she had a *man* with her. I left her with no doubts about that!

Then . . .

But I've neglected to mention an important aspect. Another house rule, apparently, for she seemed in a terrific hurry to get back downstairs. I mean, it seems she was supposed to spend only so much time with each customer and then rush him out, and that she was already running overtime with me. (Ha ha.) So she rushed about and hopped back into her blouse and skirt (all she wore, for gosh sakes!) and was hurrying out the door, when I conceived an idea I felt at the time was a brilliant one, but which later turned out to be the beginning of my misadventure proper, which, though it enriched me in experience, led to some rather startling digressions.

My thinking at this point was extremely involved, subtle, and also rapid. First, I was laughing to myself at how startled Hank would be if he ever found out how I had impressed a paid professional colored prostitute, right in her own house of ill repute, for gosh sakes! Second, I was thinking that if I could persuade her to this point, with further objective planning and action, I might continue the trend and further my extra-curricular education somewhat. I might learn even more about paid professional colored ladies by persuading her to meet me at some other time and some other place.

I was laying there wondering just how I could go about this when my idea struck. And I mean *struck*! It came like a bolt from the devine blue— the way Prof. McGillicuty says highly intellectual poetical ideas come.

My idea was, namely, this: That, in view of— First, how unintelligent and uneducated she was, and Second, how profoundly impressed she was with yours truly, (ha ha) and Third, of how easily I had charmed her several moments ago, I decided—

To tell her I was a burglar and wanted by the police and desperate for a place to hide until the heat was off.

Fantastic, I know. But that was my idea. And, lo and behold, it worked. Honest! I told her that I had been burglarizing homes in the Mount Woodstock District, and that by tracing my fingerprints the police had found me out.

This had a remarkable effect on her. She not only believed me but apparently decided I was her kind —her own underworld kind. I mean, to her mind, now that she found I was an actual criminal, for gosh sakes, she considered me a sort of friend. Well, more than just a friend, as it turned out. She went to some lengths to make sure we would meet some place else, and meet soon, and also that I would have a place to hide out. She did, in fact, (and I know this will sound just too too fantastic, but it's hard cold fact nevertheless) give me the key to her apartment.

I tell him so long, an I'm on my blackass way flyin out the door, an he grab my arm!

Yeah! I dam near leave that mothahless arm behind fore I stop. Then I draw me one bigass breath and I bout t'let that dum daddio know jes wha's on my mind, as he up an say, Hol' it, hol' it jes a secen'.

An then he babble him off some dum bullshe-it bout bein a burgler, fer Kee-ryees sake!

First, I say, Okay yer a burgler, I'm a bumblebee, but I ain got nothin fer you t'take jes now, mister burgler. I ain even got me no more fuggin time. No time a-tall!

But he still hangin on my arm an talkin an sayin he need him someplace t'hide. Yeah! He say that!

Gee-zuz! I bout t'tell him *I* is gonna need me someplace t'hide, he don' let go my arm. But I do me some o'the fastes considerin I ever in my whole poor ol Pickaninny life ever done, an I say, Man you wanna hide?

An he say, Yeah! Tha's what he wanna do.

Considerin an considerin, I don' know why he jes don' ask me my phone, but he ain done that, an he ain bout to. On'y thing I know is he ain got him no *faith*. No faith a-tall! All that mothahless jack an no faith.

But ooh-wee! I gotta do somethin. Madam gonna kick my blackass over the moon, I don' git back downstairs right now!

I say t'myseff, I say, He wanna place t'hide, an he got what it take. Dum way a-goin bout linin up a weekend, but I ain never had me no weekend trick an he got enuff so's he kin be jes's dum's he wanna be. Yeah! He got him at least one hunner, look like, an him an it ain strangers, and he ain got no faith. Long on loot, short on faith!

I say t'myseff, Girl fer that kinda jack you kin godam well believe anythin this dum Whiteboy wanna tell you.

I say, Okay Burgler, down is up. Le's go t'the moon. You wanna place t'hide, you got it.

An I tell him where I live.

Kee-ryess! I say t'myseff, Girl you in such a big-ass hurry over Madam git an git, you dam near run right past one Big Money Honey. Gee-zuz! Yer fourteen already, you gotta slow down an start in givin some.

He say he don' know where is that place I live. I tell him the number an say, Take a cab, man, take a cab. I see you in the mornin. Yeah! I see you all weekend. I say, I go back downstairs, an then I'm gonna mess roun some till you finish dressin an come on down, then I'm gonna come up t'you an I'm gonna have my partmin key in my hand. I do this, you mess roun an you jes perten like you *is* nuts, an that ain gonna be too hard! You come up t'me from behind, see, an start in nuzzlin me. You jes lean over an put

yer arms roun me an then I kin slip you my key.
Unnerstan? Okay? You dig?

He look a lil dum, but he say, Okay.

I take off, leave him t'git back in all them clothes.

Ooh-wee! This better'n waitin fer him t'call. I kin
work this big Friday night now an go on home in the
mornin an this Big Money Honey invessment gonna
be there.

Invessment? She-it! I ain got me no invessment, I
got me a whole crazy-ass bank! Yeah! No tellin
where I go from here, everythin go right.

I git downstairs, the sittin room jes fulla tricks but
I can' go up now. No!

I scoot like somebody lit my tail, right on back
t'the dressin room, an make s'if I is gonna powder up
some more. Madam see me go but she too busy t'do
anythin right now. Tricks jes a-streamin in.

I git my key outta my purse an start peekin out
thru the curtin, waitin fer my Big Money Honey. He
bout take all night.

But he make it. I see him standin there, lookin dum,
an I scoot back out t'the sittin room an he do like I
tol' him. He ack dum an start sayin he wanna go
back upstairs wiff me an while we is funnin like that,
I slip him my key.

I say, Nex time, Lover.

He say, Okay, nex time.

An he take off out the door.

Phew! Invessment ain easy t'git.

Burgler? Kee-ryess!

Trouble! Gee-zuz! Course he got trouble. Wiff
that wad, course he got nothin but trouble.

I on my swingin ass way back upstairs wiff another College Joe, I say t'myseff, Burgler you jes go on home t'my place an hide yerseff cozy. Don' you go nowhere else, man. I git home, we gonna talk some real sweet weekend bizness t'begin wiff, then we gonna settle down t'invessment. An who know what that gonna lead to!

Kee-ryess! How come one cat git her ass so lucky so fast? Way he finger that wad, I *know*, I jes dee-diddly-dam well *know* this invessment gonna be long an happy.

Outside the ill repute house again, this time with her key in my pocket, I paused a moment for some hard, bold, analytical thinking. I thought: Good grief, JC! Have you by any chance, somewhere between nine o'clock and now, become guilty of rationalization?

But the answer, of course, was an emphatic No. After all, I honestly owed this little escapade to my education. I mean, a formal education is one thing, but there are, after all, a few things one doesn't learn inside a classroom. And closely and objectively inspecting the environment and activity of one colored lady of ill repute (both professional) was something which would certainly stand me in good stead later on in life. Besides, I'm inclined to think that Dad must have had some similar experience when he was young, or else how could he be so sophisticated and well equipped for his outside job on the town obscenity board? (Outside office and hospital, that is.)

Added to that—the fact that she believed my fantastic burglar story and had slipped me the key to her apartment and wanted me to hide out there (no doubt in an illicit living arrangement with her) and that such circumstances do not present themselves often (ha ha), I felt practically obliged to follow through.

And find out what I could. Which, up to the present time, had been plenty. About such paid professional ladies, I mean, and specifically in exactly which ways and by which methods they are different, and morally cancerous.

The big immediate danger being, of course, venereal disease. But even Dad has told me that professional prostitutes are very careful about disease, and Hank has constantly beaten on my ears about how the colored girls who work in houses of ill repute inspect each customer and wash his certain unprintable parts, and also see a doctor regularly. (I doubt Hank's word about them seeing a doctor regularly, for gosh sakes. I can't imagine a waiting room full of such ladies. But she did inspect me.) (Carefully.) So I decided to remain undaunted and carry on. After all, it isn't every day, as I've pointed out, that a student gets an opportunity outside the classroom to learn firsthand the really substandard side of life. (Though I'm fully aware, that in my case at least, it was less an opportunity than the result of my own quick thinking and natural endowments which had led me to my present pass.)

So, it was *Hup* two three four, *Hup* two three four, back up that dark street, meeting this virtual mob of fellows climbing out of cars and walking, probably students, going in the opposite direction, until I reemerged on the avenue. There to pause for one short moment—again teetering on the brink of indecision.

I thought : Should you, James Cartwright Holland, really actually *go* there? Or would it be better to toss this educational opportunity to the winds and return to the frat house?

Then a taxi came towards me and I hailed it, and I thought : No, you have nothing to do—absolutely nothing—until Monday morning. Why miss a sociological opportunity which may leave you wiser in every way? And, after all, you are a normal male human being with normal appetites, and it will be a long time before you go home again and can see Margie or Susie.

Also, I thought of my flunking grades—biology, psychology, French—and how angry Dad was going to be when he found out about them, and what a rough second half semester I was up against.

Good grief! I had really never stopped to consider the seriousness of the matter—flunking out, I mean. I thought : Imagine you, JC, flunked out—disowned by friends and family, a bum, an actual bum—an outcast, even, sneaking about in neighborhoods such as this one, picking food from garbage cans, ending by dying tragically in a gutter some place. Holy Christmas!

One big wild unlikely weekend (of field study, so to speak) (or, if you please, cultural exchange) with a paid professional lady (colored), then it's back to the books, this time in earnest.

Well, anyway, the taxi stopped and I bounced in and gave him the address she had given me. Off we went. And I'll certainly admit it—I was glad to be back inside a taxi and on my way out of that neighborhood. As we went past the Black-n-Tan, those

Negro fellows were still standing there, doing nothing. Except that it seemed a couple of them were staring, for gosh sakes, at me. That bunch of loafers made me shudder. I don't mean that I'm prejudiced, but I don't understand how they can just stand and stand and do absolutely nothing for minute after minute, hour after hour. I suppose, though, that it's racial. I mean, what other explanation could there be? And just the other day, one frat brother was talking about his army experience and he claims many Negroes make very poor soldiers—made a poor record in the Great War, don't follow orders well at all—so I suppose you just can't get away from it, it's racial. Them standing there doing nothing, I mean.

But I had happier thoughts to think, for the taxi was going in the general direction of the university —back to the only part of this god-forsaken town I know anything about. Not that I'm completely familiar with that section, but at least it's civilized. It may not be friendly, like my own hometown, but it's civilized. I'll say that for it. So the closer we got to it, the better I felt about the entire proposition. Until— Bamb!

We drove right smack dab into it! Then I began to get a little worried. I thought : Impossible! She can't live here, can she? In a dormitory, or something? (Ha ha.) Christmas!

But as it turned out, I didn't have a worry in the world. On that score. We drove right on through the university section of the city and kept right on going into a part of town I'd never even seen before. Then we made some fancy turns and zigzaggings which completely lost me—up one street, left for half a block, right for two blocks, left again, and so forth, until—Bamb again!

Here we are at some huge apartment house with a canopy, for gosh sakes, out over the sidewalk! Christmas! Holy Christmas! I mean, it wasn't a new apartment house, exactly, and it certainly wasn't as swank as, say, a Park Avenue address or anything like *that*, but it was a far cry from what I had expected. (Though I can't really say what I had expected, for I had no specific expectation.) The point is, I didn't expect *this*!

Well, I paid the driver, tipping him judiciously, just in case, and strolled on in, as if I knew what I was doing. (Ha ha.) Fortunately, there wasn't a soul in sight. What was in sight was this lobby affair with overstuffed chairs and that stuff here and there, a huge long wooden table and about the biggest wall mirror I've ever seen anywhere. And that carpet! Wow! I thought: Christmas, JC! Before you get to the elevator, you're liable to drown for gosh sakes!

But I made it.

Needless to say, perhaps. The point is that . . . Well, I might as well admit it. What I mean to say is, right here, due to a slight oversight, I panicked. I pushed the button for the elevator and panicked. I thought : What the heck apartment am I supposed to be going to anyway? You see, I didn't even know her name, let alone the number of her apartment.

What to do, what to do.

I thought of hunting up the janitor and describing her to him in the hope that he could direct me, but —I *mean*! It wasn't like I was on my way to see an old friend who had recently moved. She was non-white, so certainly the janitor would also be non-white. And she was an ill repute at that. In view of these matters, and even though the place was sort of fancy, I mean far from decrepit, who knows what I'd encounter in the form of a janitor?

(Right about here, I should add that that place knocked me out! I mean, I somehow had gotten the idea that prostitution and slums went hand in hand, so prostitutes lived, like a hand in a glove, in slums. Well, I was learning.)

But meanwhile—what the heck to do. The elevator arrived and I stood there looking at it for awhile, then turned away. I thought: Good gracious, JC, should you go all the way back to that ill repute house and ask her her name and apartment number? But, good grief, the taxi had cost me two dollars and fifty cents, counting the tip. Five bucks that would be. No, seven-fifty, by the time I got back. I mean, it's only money, *but*!

Of course all this trouble was due to my slight oversight. I hadn't looked at the key she'd given me.. Once I did, my worries were over, so to speak. It said, 'Apt. 404.'

Silly, what little oversights can lead to.

So up I went to the fourth floor, got off and found Room 404. I mean, Apt. 404. And, yes, the key unlocked the door. I found the light switch and—Bamb!

What a place she had! Wow! I mean! Christmas!

You went in and right off the bat, there, just inside the door was this huge mat, like a Japanese mat. To the left of that was this little foyer affair with shoes on the floor and coats hanging up. I got the

point. I took off my shoes and left them in that little
foyer. I have a quick mind for such things.

Besides, you'd have to be pretty stupid to wear
shoes past that mat because that rug—wow! Such a
rug! Permit me one gross understatement: It was
white. I mean, WHITE. Pure white! Hollywood
white! Matter of fact, the whole entire place seemed
like something out of Hollywood. The big white rug,
wall to wall, and feeling sort of made of feathers, and
then these walls—sky blue, with paintings, for gosh
sakes, like from Mexico, hanging on them. And, on
the far wall, this great tremendous curtain hanging
from ceiling to floor and wall to wall. (It covered
a big picture window, I was soon to learn.) Then, for
furniture, there were these low coffeetables. I mean,
low! And big. Sort of a dark purple color. Something like that. And then, this couch. As big as a bed,
it looked. Matter of fact, it looked more like a bed
than a couch, except that it had a backrest and arms
and separate cushions and all.

But that wasn't all. The entire place was fantastic!
(Oh I realize it was gaudy, but I mean, it wasn't what
I had expected. It was also swanky, even if it was
gaudy.) The white rug went right on into this bedroom and in there, there was another one of those
bed-couch affairs, but this one had a pink counter-
pane and pillows, and so I was forced to conclude it
was, in fact, a bed, no stuff. It had to be a bed, you
see, because there were only three rooms and a bathroom, and the third room was a kitchen. (Also fantastic!)

Well, I ran around for awhile, inspecting, looking
everything over well, trying to convince myself I had

the key to such an apartment, given to me by the girl (even if she was colored) who lived here. It hardly seemed possible. In fact, in strict matter of hard cold fact, it seemed unbelievable! But, I managed to get acclimatized finally, and settled in the bedroom because she had this tremendous hi fi in there. I felt in the mood, about that time, for some nice smooth semi-classics, but I soon discovered she (but after all, she can't help being unintelligent and uneducated, and so lacking in good taste) had nothing but jazz records. But wow! Did she have plenty of those! Stacks and stacks of nothing but jazz on labels I'd never even heard of, for gosh sakes, by artists I'd never even heard of. But, I discovered how the hi fi worked and put on a stack. Then I took off my suit and shirt and hung them neatly in her closet (equally fantastic!) and flopped down on her bed.

I thought: JC my friend, pinch yourself. You may be dreaming!

Mornin, I git home, he's there. Yeah! He leave the door unlatch.

Big Money Honey sleepin in my bed.

Sometime, mornin, I watch tee vee. I watch the man put the numbers on the map. Sep this mornin, the man ain on, cause it's Saterday.

She-it!

Right now, what I shoulda done, I shoulda got me my weekend hunner. I shoulda wake him up an got my loot. Madam say, Git the cash first.

Yeah! I shoulda, but I di'n'. Jackie say, invessment is give an git, give an git.

Trouble is, I still don' know what-the-fug fer sure. Maybe he gonna be invessment, maybe he jes gonna be a weekend. Maybe he gonna take off an I ain gonna see him no more. I bout tween a she-it and a sweat an a give an a git.

But I say t'myseff, Girl one thing sure. Him an that wad ain strangers, so ain no use you gittin too greedy too quick. Jes relax an maybe you end up hittin the jackpot. Yeah! I say t'myseff, Girl maybe you got you a whole fuggin Rockafellah! She-it, you don' know. Play it cool an find out.

Sep, on'y one trouble. This poor ol cat is draggin ass. Yeah! Friday big night.

Lazy pussy ain gonna do nobody no good, I know. But a sore pussy ain gonna do nobody no good neither. I put my poor ol blackass in that bed, hard t'tell wha's gonna happen, him sleepin like he is. On'y he give me a chance t'sleep an git some naecher back, we kin have us some nice fun. Later.

Nex, I find it ain gonna be easy. Jackie say, Invessment real simple, nothin to it.

Gonna haff t'straighten Jackie out some.

I haff way int'bed, my Big Money Honey pop up like the whole worl' comin t'the end. Yeah! He sit up right now! He say, like, he say, Wha, Who, Hee, Ho!

He jittery agen.

I say, Sweet Baby it's on'y me.

An then, trouble trouble trouble.

First, he take off his unnerwear. Yeah! He been sleepin in his unnerwear. Gee-zuz!

Then he give me this crap-happy smile, an then he start in grabbin my ass like he wanna have me fer breakfes'.

I say, Whoa Baby! I say, Sweet Lover, hol' the phone! I say, Man ain you got no considerashun? I been workin my poor ol ass all night long! Kee-ryess! Pussy ain made o'steel. Hol' off a lil, an later on we kin have us a real nice time. I say, Cool it, Lover, put that mean nasty tiger back in his cage an let me git some sleep. Okay?

But he ain buyin none o'that. No-oh-oh! This good mornin daddio wanna do nothin but go! Yeah!

I keep on tryin t'be real nice an talk soff. I say,

Lay back down, Wildman. Lay back down an I fix you up good.

But he so fuggin square his head got corners. He don' hear nothin I say. He frisky's a tomcat wiffout ears an twicet's nasty.

Gee-zuz! I too tired t'fight, too tired t'fug, an he ain fer talkin. Trouble trouble trouble!

I can' help it, I lose my cottinpickin head. I quit talkin soff an I say, You crap-happy fay mothahfuggin son-a-bitch! Fer Kee-ryees sake man! Git off me an go t'sleep. Can' you see I ain got no naecher leff?

He quit, okay. But then he go t'layin there lookin real hurt. He wrinkle up an jes look hurt.

She-it! I can' git no sleep, him lookin like that. Sides I ain got no right t'treat no trick like that.

I say, Okay Lover, you win. One more ain gonna kill me. I spose.

An I give this one las' Friday job all the snap I got leff. I like t'break my poor ol blackass, but I do.

Know what he do? That dum she-it stop right in the middle an he cuss me out! Yeah! He start in givin me hell fer goin good, an he tell me t'do like I *feel* like doin.

Gee-zuz! He plain nuts!

I say—nice's I kin—I say, Okay Lover, I *feel* like sleepin.

So I lay like dead, and he go t'jammin an rammin.

Then he roll off an go t'sleep, an I dam well do the same. I sleep like I ain livin.

Nex, all this stompin an bangin an bumpin upstairs wake us boff up, an right now my Whiteboy pop up like a mothahjumpin jack-in-a-box an hop outta bed. Yeah! He pop an hop an go runnin roun like

he bout t'fly. Firs' thing I know, he climb int'his
pants like he wanna take off fer the moon.

I say t'myseff, Whooops! This ain gonna do no
good.

First he wanna wham bam my poor old worn out
me t'death, then he wanna run off an leave me wiffout
even payin. Yeah! He wanna take that wad an *go*!

I bout t'lose my Pickaninny head agen an scratch
his eyes out, but I don'. I see he is mostly jittery, tha's
all. He scared o'that bumpin upstairs.

On'y one thing t'do. I haul ass outta bed an baby
him up some more. I gotta tell him ain nothin but
noise upstairs, nothin t'git jittery bout.

He say, Wha's all that noise come from?

I say, She-it, I don' know. Ain nothin but noise is
all.

He say, He think this a nice place an noise, like,
ain *right* here.

I tell him, Sure this a nice place, but noise is noise
anyplace.

See, Francine, she live straight up. I don' tell this
mothah that, but I say t'myseff, That Francine's at it
agen. She got that girlfrien' wiff her an they is puttin
on a show.

Like, Francine, she got this one White girlfrien'
come in an raise hell. They puts on shows fer tricks
sometime, an sometime they puts on shows fer nobody.
They puttin on a show fer nobody is causin all that
bumpin. But I don' tell my invessment that. I don' tell
him nothin I don' gotta tell him.

Pritty soon he see I ain scared, he feel better. He
take off his pants an hang 'em up agen. He do this,
I try t'see, is his wad still in 'em, but I can' tell fer

sure, and I don' wanna ack greedy an reach in his pocket right in front o'him.

I say, Piss on that noise, Lover. Le's sleep.

But he say he don' wanna sleep no more.

I tell him I do.

He say, Okay, sleep.

I do. I so dam tired, I jes go right back t'sleep an don' even give a toot bout him prowlin roun my partmin.

Nex time I wake up, he got them pants on agen. He jes standin in the doorway, lookin at me, wearin them pants. I don' know why he figure he gotta put on clothes, but sure's hell he's wearin them pants.

On'y one good thing bout that. I kin see the lump his wad's makin in his pants. Yeah! I kin see that pritty lil ol lump jes plain's day. I say t'myseff, Well at least he ain tryin t'pull no cheat.

Then I say, Hey Lover, how come you dress?

He say, I ain dress!

Gee-zuz! I don' know what he calls it.

I say, You is too dress!

He say, He ain. He say, All I got on's my pants. Kee-ryess!

I say, Sweet Baby, whatta you call pants? You don' need no pants here. I say, Sweetheart, take 'em off an leave me hang 'em up real nice agen.

He say, Wha, Who, Hee, Ho! He say, He ain got him no unnerwear on, or nothin!

I say, She-it! So what?

He say—like, he make dum noises—an he say, He git chilly, he run roun wiffout nothin on.

Gee-zuz!

I say, Oh no, Sugar. Jes open the curtin on the

winda an we git us some sunshine, keep us warm, an then we kin do us a lil Adam an Eve.

He say, Who, Wha, Ho, Hee! Agen he say like that. An he stan there lookin dum fer a minit. But he do, he open the curtin. Then he come back an take his wad-happy pants off an hang 'em up real nice.

Ooh-wee! That wad make me feel good! He hangin, I wanna hop outta bed an help. Sep, I don' wanna look greedy an ack nasty, so I stay put.

He done hangin, I git up. We jes fuss roun, him playin my records an me goin an gittin me a bath.

I'm in the tub, he wanna know does I want him t'wash my back.

Hee hee!

I say, Sure Honey, sure!

He do. Yeah! He wash real nice. Feel good. He done, I lay back down in the tub an start in talkin t'myseff bout all that jack. I snooze some, doin that.

Then he come back an wake me up an ask don' I never eat.

I say, Hell yeah, I eat.

He say, Crissmiss! When?

He alla time sayin crissmiss.

I say, Right now I'm gonna cut yer cute cock off an fry him, man. Whatta you thinka that?

He laugh. He doin okay. Bout now, it seem pritty nice havin a rich White loverboy roun here. Long's he kin pay.

He wanna know, I gonna make us breakfes?

Gee-zuz! He coulda make us breakfes while he was fartin roun here. But I don' say that. I say, Ain you gonna make us breakfes?

He look dum agen. I git outta the tub and dry off

an start makin breakfes. I fry eight eggs, an he say he thinks tha's too many. He make a noise like a chicken. But he eat bout six o'them eggs.

Then he wanna know how old I am. I tell him sixteen. Couple-a years don' hurt nothin. Nobody take me fer fourteen anyhow, less I tell 'em. An Madam say, Tell 'em eighteen. Too much law trouble, bein fourteen. But Gee-zuz! Time I git t'be eighteen, I wanna retire, have me some fun fer myseff.

He say, He is *nine*teen!

I say, So what!

He say, So nothin. Ab'slootly nothin!

Then he wanna know my name, so I tell him Kitten.

I say, Wha's yer name?

He say, Jimmy.

Yeah! Jimmy! Hee hee! Jimmy the Burgler!

Nex, I git him t'do the dishes. He don' wanna, but I sweet talk him an play him int'doin them anyhow.

An that gives me my chance. I go back, sneak a look in his pants. Yeah! I count fast! Over one hunner. Okay, I feel better an better, now I know he kin pay real easy fer the whole weekend. I ain tol' him t'pay yet, but I wanna know he kin, anyhow. Sides, maybe he turn out t'be invessment fer sure an I don' gotta ask him t'pay fer no lousy weekend. He be my invessment, he kin jes pay what he want when he wanna.

I git all fuss up, thinkin all that loot an how him an it such real good frien's. I say t'myseff, Girl, time t'do you some givin so's you kin do you some gittin later. Tha's how invessment work, ain it? Okay, start givin!

I git t'feelin so good, I say t'myseff, Girl you need

a lil rest anyhow, why don' you call Madam an knock off fer the weekend, now you sure he kin pay. Yeah! Give my Big Money Honey a fine time steada lookin down all them Saterday night one-eyes.

I say, Honey how bout I knock off fer the weekend?

He say, Huh?

Ooh-wee Skinny Minnie! Whatta moon-goin muddlefug!

He say, Off work?

I say, Yeah Sugar, off work.

He say, Yeah yeah yeah!

So I call Madam on the phone. I say, Madam I'm sick.

She say, She-it!

I say, I be in Monday night, gotta take off t'night an Sunday.

She say, Girl you lie! She git mad an say it gonna be a big Saterday night, she needs me. She say, She kin tell I ain sick way I say it.

Piss on Madam. Me an my Big Money Honey gonna start us up one fine invessment. We gonna be frien's. I tell Madam I'm sick an tha's that! I say it so's she kin tell I needs a rest.

She say, Okay but she don' like it none a-tall.

Then I feel good. I feel better an better. I lay down on my nice rug wiff couple-a pillas unner my head an watch my Big Money Honey doin dishes. I watch the cheeks o'his ass movin. He got a pritty ass.

He finish, he load up the recordplayer agen, an then he lay down too. We jes a-layin in the sunshine on my nice rug feelin good, lissenin t'the music.

Sep, I kin tell he ain lissenin *to* it. He lissenin *at*

it. I spect he jes don' dig color' music. He's too fay
White.

But he doin okay, anyhow.

Everythin fine now, an I kin even feel myseff gittin
back a lil naecher. Yeah! He lookin pritty good bout
now.

I say t'myseff, I say, Girl you ain turn' on fer over
a whole week. Work work work an gittin no good fun
fer yerseff, is what you been doin, Girl. No wonner
you ain got much pep.

I say t'myseff, I kin git Big Money Honey t'do him
some o'his jam bammin at the right time, I kin turn on
hotass good. Yeah! An we got us all weekend t'play
nice an fetch us some high flyin too.

Hot dam!

I say, Hey Adam, you gotta lil ol apple you wanna
give Eve?

But he jes look dum agen. Kee-ryess!

Insprashun! Yeah, he need him some insprashun.
Put us boff in a cross-country mood.

So I git up an git my pitchers. Make me feel good,
thinkin how he gonna feel when he see my pitchers.
Ooh-wee! I like them pitchers too. I got 'em took by
this fotograffer, pay me fifty. He takes 'em someplace,
sells 'em. But he give me some first, an I like t'look
at 'em oncet in awhile. I was younger when they
was took, got me more titty now. But I ain
gotta wear no bra like Francine gotta. Course, Francine, she ain nothing but a sassy-ass has-been. She
dam near thirty.

I puts the girl-girl ones on the bottom an the ones
wiff the Whiteman on top, an I come back. He sittin
a-gin the divan smokin an dreamin an lissenin t'the

music. He lookin prittier an prittier. Lil ol Johnny-cock jes a-hangin loose an layin on the rug. Ain gonna lay like that fer long. Hee hee !

I say, Hey Baby, look here !

He do.

Oncet I show these pitchers t'Bennie an he like t'turn me inside out !

Big Money Honey lookin, up come that cute lil ol thing, jes nice's kin be. Then he look at me an ack bashful, like. Then he do him some more pitcher lookin.

I say, Hey Jimmy the Burgler, you figure on jimmy-in somethin wiff that?

An I say, Hey Sweet Sugar Loverboy Honey, what you got in mind t'do wiff that cute lil thing?

An Kee-ryess ! Fore I know it, I stuck my foot in it. Yeah ! I hurt his feelings, jes talkin an funnin like that, I hurt his fuggin feelins. I don' mean to, but I do. Fer a minit, I don' know what in the wide-ass worl' I do t'hurt him, but I sure know I do. He lookin hurter an hurter, an then he lookin mean !

Gee-zuz ! I say, Baby wha's-a matter?

An bout the time I say that, I know wha's-a matter. But fore I kin fix it up, he's off an runnin dum agen.

He say—real loud an mad, like—he say, *Lil* ! He say, what the hell you mean, lil !

He say it, like, LIT till. Is how he say it. He start in shoutin bout how it ain LIT till.

Trouble trouble trouble. This fuggin invessment ain nothin but trouble. Alla time misunnerstan. Gee-zuz ! I shoulda knowed I can' joke wiff this dum bastid. Madam alla time sayin, All fay tricks the same that way. Never say lil. Always say, Oooh what a big

big one you got. An then say, Wow! An carry on. That make 'em feel good.

I shoulda knowed, but right now it seem t'me my Big Money Honey got him such a nice—such a *big* nice one, I jes plain fergit.

Anyhow, I jes lissen t'his shoutin fer a time, then I shout back. I say, Shut up! Yeah! I say, Jimmy you dum doe-doe, jes hol' yer yip-yappin mothah-jumpin jaw a minit, will ya?

He do.

I say, Baby what the hell you think I am? Pussy from nose t'toes? An I say, Baby what I was tryin t'say, I was tryin t'say you got a *pritty* one. It ain fer Kee-ryess sake LIT til, it's jes right. Okay? So what the hell you want, a phonepole?

Then he smile an git t'feelin better.

I say, Gee-zuz, man! We got all weekend!

An he jes look dum.

I say t'myseff, This dum mothah ack like he wanna do nice but he jes don' know how. Kee-ryess! Kin he be *that* dum? Don' he know better'n t'ack tough and hurry-up when it's time fer playin slow an pritty? Maybe he think he starin in movies, playin Jack the Ripper or somethin. I say t'myseff, Girl one thing sure, he ain gonna turn you on playin he's the dog an yer the bone.

Then I git me an idea. I ack nice an play slow an pritty, show him, ack it out fer him, maybe he quit playin Jack the Ripper. Maybe.

I try. I play roun the worl' on him real soff an slow an nice, like I think he's made o'cottin candy.

Then he ack like he wanna play back, an I guess maybe he got the idea now, so I let him go at it.

But Gee-zuz! Wrong agen! He jes a-huffin an puffin an grabbin an scratchin an toothin like he think we still in the cathouse an short on time.

This ain no good, so I call him off. I say, Whoa! I say, Hol' up right here, Jack! Rare back, man this ballgame's all over.

He say, Wha, Who, Hee, Ho! He look real up in the air.

I say, Gee-zuz, man! Ain I got you slow' down yet?

An he say, Huh?

She-it.

I say t'myseff, Girl it gittin plainer an plainer this mothah jes can' play nice an slow. Kee-ryess! How come I got my ass stuck wiff such a dum invessment? Jackie alla time sayin how nice she and her White-loverman git along, an I gotta go an git me this dum she-it, can' play nice. He ain never never gonna turn me on playin that dum way. I don' know how one Whiteboy kin be so dum's t'wanna play turnabout, then go an ack mean, but this daddio jes that dum.

I git t'considerin agen. I consider how he can' even lissen t'music. He play like he lissens. He go t'play, he know *what* t'do, he don' know *how* t'do. Music he lissen *at* it steada *to* it.

She-it! He jes too mothahfuggin fay. He too White, boff inside an out.

Sep, plain t'see he wanna play. An I dam well want me some funnin too.

I try agen. I try teechin him, talkin t'him jes like he was a lil chile. Yeah! I gotta Un-learn him, an then I gotta Re-learn him.

I say, Baby you wanna turn me on?

He say, Yeah yeah yeah; Tha's what he gonna do.

I say, *Gonna* do! Oh no, Baby, no you ain gonna.
Not the way you been doin.

He say, Huh?

I say, Man like this grunt thumpin stuff go fine at
the right time, but this ain it. You dig?

He say, Huh?

I say, Like right now is time fer slow an easy. You
dig?

An he still jes on'y say nothin but *Huh*!

Ooh-wee!

I say, Like man, we got us all weekend, see.

An he say, Yeah yeah yeah.

I say, Okay. We got time t'fetch us some good fun
by playin slow an nice. An I say, But we ain gonna
make it, you keep up yer fuggin huffin an puffin an
mothahrammin railroadin.

An he jes say Huh agen.

But I keep on. I say, Sweetheart you gotta learn
t'play pritty, you wanna fetch us boff a good time.
I say, like, good time gotta be foun first. Like we
gotta coax him out. Good time is bashful, like. You dig?
You ain never gonna fetch him out by bein hurry-up
an hurtful, an huffin and puffin an toothin an scratchin like you been doin. Yeah! Good time so bashful,
he gonna hide on you, you do like that. Yeah! You
wanna make him come out an chase us, you gotta
ack pritty. You ack nice an play soff an slow an pritty,
then yer gonna fetch him out an he gonna find us.
Yeah! He finds us, an then he takes over, see? Oncet
he out an foun us, then he chase us, an then he catch
us, an then he takes over. An then, man, we is flyin!
An when we gits t'flyin, then you kin go t'huffin an

puffin an wham bam jam fuggin all you wanna. Yeah!
But first, we gotta coax. Dig?

An Gee-zuz! He still jes look dum's ever.

Oh my poor ol blackass Pickaninny me, how come
I pick me such a dum invessment firs' time out? I
say t'myseff, Girl ain no use. This dum she-it don'
wanna turn you *on*, he wanna turn you *off*!

Nex, I jes a-sittin an feelin bad, he come over an
start in. On'y this time, I kin tell he's tryin t'do like
I tol' him. So I keep on tellin. I talk pritty, I say, Go
easy, Lover. Play pritty an nice an talk t'that lil ol
titty real soff. Yeah!

He do. An he git t'doin much better. Pritty soon,
he's doin real fine.

Fack, he git t'doin me good's ever I been done. He
goin norff an souff, an eas' an wes', and he goin this
way real sweet. He treatin me like fine an dandy, an
I git t'feelin like chocklit candy! Hot dam! My
teechin pay off real fine!

Nex, why sweet singin Kee-ryess almighty, I shift
gears! Yeah! My bumblebee goes an gits him a lil
french honey an I toot my whistle! Yeah! He got me
lit up an flipfloppin, like he's the cat an I'm the trick.
An Ooh-wee Skinny Minnie! Pritty soon, I'm movin
on magic!

I let him know I dee-diddly-dam well on my flip-
pin-ass way, and when he hop in that ol saddle, he
got my naecher up so skyhigh, all I kin do is hang on
an go. Yeah! Bout now, all the slam bam jam fuggin
this daddio kin ever do jes fine by me. Cause we is
flyin! Yeah! Ol man good time done caught us an he
is rollin us yonder! An here we go, jes a-wingdingin
somethin awful, jes a-drivin home like we boff gonna

flip, and right now he is so everlovin sweet an fine,
I dam near fergit he got jack!

Nex, homerun! Yeah! Boff us pop like the forff
of July! I like t'come clean outta my black hide an
he done huff an puff his way t'hell an back! Ain never
been two bellybuttons no tighter!

Lil while later, he start in movin ass agen, like he
wanna go git us one more. I say t'myseff, Girl time
t'put on the brakes. This sweet bumblebee got him
jes bout all the honey he kin git fer now, don' want
him wearin hiseff alla way out. We got us all weekend. Yeah!

Sides, Madam alla time sayin, Don' never wear 'em
clean out all at oncet. Springtime don' come at no
sixty mile an hour!

So I call him off. I don' specially wanna, but I do.
I gits t'thinkin bout all that jack, an bout what
Madam say, an, like, nother thing Madam say, she
say, Wornout pecker ain no good fer payin up!

Christmas! You'd think an intelligent, red-blooded, white, church-going non-communist like I, with my genius for great salesmanship, would avoid ending up in the nude. After having cleverly connived his way into the afore-mentioned unbelievable position, that is, I mean, the colored prostitute (paid) and her swank apartment (fantastic). But, as it turned out, that's what happened. Nude, I mean. I ended up in the nude.

And that isn't all that happened. Christmas! Would that I could decently tell all! (Ha ha.) But I can't. Not in detail, for gosh sakes! I mean, I'll sort of rough it out, like in a novel of high literary merit.

And since I'm a fellow who puts plenty of stock in hard cold fact, I'll begin at the logical beginning. The beginning of the episode following those I've already covered.

Well, I flopped down on her bed to listen to her collection of strange unheard of jazz records, and did this in my shorts and tee shirt. Secondly, I fell asleep. (I hadn't realized how dogtired I was until then.) I woke up sometime during the wee hours of that fateful morning (the music having gone off automatically) and crawled under the covers, and was sacked out dead to the world, when—Bamb!

You know how it is when you wake up suddenly in some strange bed. You forget where you are and start looking around for the old familiar objects. Well, I woke up and expected to see my room in the frat house. But instead I see this stark naked girl (colored) climbing into bed beside me. So it took me a second to acclimatize myself and realize just what the heck was going on.

Then I remembered the night before and all, and how she had believed my wild lie about being a burglar and wanted by the police and society, and so had given me her key and realized that here I was—being kept (I mean pretending to be kept) by a paid professional colored prostitute. Well, obviously, what I should have done at this juncture was taken up on my investigation where I had left off, carrying it further—on into the realms of functional anthropology, even, but since I hadn't had my eight winks yet, and since her bed was so darn comfortable, and . . . (well, everything else included) I didn't do that, right off.

In order to maintain my high literary plain, I won't of course, go into detail about what I did do. Right off the bat, I mean, when she climbed into bed beside me. (Except to mention that I figured I had sort of a score to settle with that paid professional, now that she was home and not working and all, and with me, whom she considered a fellow underworld character.) (And to add that I let her know she had a man with her, a real manly man.)

Following which we retired to slumber.

(I might also add—though I don't wish to dwell unduly on this matter—that she tried to act reluctant when she first came home. Imagine! A professional, for gosh sakes, acting reluctant!) (But that only added spice, of course.) (Once she stopped using her foul language, that is.)

Well, I was feeling knocked out and sleeping pretty hard and too deep in the sack to give a hoot where I was—for the moment—when, along about mid-morning—Bamb!

All of a sudden this gosh awful pounding woke me. I mean! It sounded like the whole entire upstairs was going to cave in on us any second! I don't know what the heck it was all about, but it came from the apartment directly over hers—like somebody up there didn't like us and was pounding through with a sledge hammer. Or something.

Well, before I knew exactly what I was doing, I had leaped out of bed and was scrambling into my clothes. After all, I wasn't the right color for that apartment house, so I wasn't about to register a complaint with the management. I thought : Sister, I'll see you later. I'll get your phone number on my way out of here and call you up sometime when the heat's off. Right now, this is no place for a burglar like me. I mean, at that moment all sorts of ideas were in my head. I even had visions of a police raid on that apartment house, for gosh sakes, and her telling the police I was a burglar and hiding out, and the police believing her. (I mean, stranger things have happened.)

But at this point, she started acting like some gun moll (very tan) in some gangster's life who didn't

want her man to leave. She jumped out of bed and
started trying to pull the clothes off me as fast as I
pulled them on. And all the time jabbering away in
her dialect so fast that, with all that noise from upstairs, I couldn't understand a word she was saying.
All I knew for sure was that she thought the noise
was nothing to worry about, that it was sort of a
regular occurrence, and that it would stop after a
while.

Which, incidentally, it did. But before it did, I gave
up the fight and decided to stay. If all that thump-
ing and crashing didn't bother her (and to prove it
didn't she went right back to sleep) I figured it
shouldn't bother me. So I didn't let it.

But it had thoroughly wakened me. I can say that
for it. I gave sleeping one more try but found myself
all slept out, so I got up and just browsed around.
I hunted for a morning paper, but didn't find one.
Then I switched on her TV and watched one of those
classic old westerns, and when it was over and still
she continued to sleep, I took a shower. (Also a fantastic thing, that shower. Sunken tub, huge pink
turkish towels longer than she was tall, for gosh
sakes! Mirrors all over the place, the works.) (I should
add, I also thought taking a shower would wake her,
but no such luck. When I stepped back into the bedroom she was sleeping like a log.)

So I considered raiding her kitchen for something
to eat. However, I refrained from this—being sus-
picious that such an act might break some tribal taboo,
or something, and also confident that she'd come to
sooner or later and would be hungry herself, etc.

But there was nothing to do to pass the time. I

mean, there was nothing on TV worth watching after that western, and her livingroom was absolutely bare of things to read. Not a magazine or newspaper in the place. Not one! So, finally, around noon, I woke her up. I didn't know her name at that point, so I just kept calling, 'Hey, come on. Hey, get up. Hey you, it's noon, time to get up.' But she didn't budge until I yanked her big toe.

Finally, she sat up, rubbed her eyes, smiled and looked at yours truly. Then—Bamb!

Right off the bat, she got all excited about me wearing my trousers. Well, I didn't know what to do. I was flabbergasted! My trousers, for crying out loud, was all that I had on!

I thought: This woman is unbelievable! In fact, she's downright Bohemian! Possibly even Beatnik!

Even when I told her all I had on was my trousers, she insisted I take them off and parade around, for crying out loud, in the complete and utter nude!

Well, I'm far from being a prude. (Of course, ha ha, or how could I find myself in such a situation.) But on the other hand, I'm no nudist colony faddist either. I mean, I'm *normal*! I'm just a regular guy and not used to parading around strange apartments without a stitch on. In broad daylight, yet! Still, in keeping with my original detecting and consequently functional anthropologist motif, I figured, what the heck, when in Rome . . .

So I took my trousers off and hung them back up in her bedroom closet, and that made her feel better. And there I was, parading around that strange non-white apartment in the utter and absolute nude, without a stitch on.

Which seemed pretty silly at first, but gradually I acclimatized myself to the idea and anyway she did the same—just walked around as if it were the most natural thing in the world to go about as bare as the day you were born, for gosh sakes!

And everything went along pretty good for a time. She took a bath and then made breakfast (another fantastic thing—eight eggs, for crying out loud! Eight! Four apiece. With bacon and sausage, the works.) Christmas! I was darn near starving to death by the time we got around to eating that breakfast, but I didn't expect to make an all-day feast on nothing *but* breakfast!

After breakfast, she started in clowning around and jabbering in her uneducated lingo about me doing the dishes. I tried to tell her that I don't do dishes, but she kept clowning and the next thing I knew she had tied a little apron around my waist and shoved me in front of the sink.

Well, it's strange: That apron came as such a relief to my nudity that I didn't fight it, I just started in doing dishes (not exactly a habit with me, doing dishes) and she skipped off to the livingroom, etc.

Then, a little later, she wanted to know if I'd like her not to go to her ill repute house that night. I said I thought that would be okay, so she called the syndicate. (I know from reading reliable reports that these ill repute houses are controlled by a gigantic crime syndicate, so I surmised it was the syndicate she called. Maybe the Mafia, even.) And she told them she was sick. (They too, have their employer-employee rules, regulations and relations, no doubt.)

Well, for awhile I didn't know what the heck she

had in mind, but I soon found out. I caught sight of her (out of the corner of my eye while I did dishes) laying on her rug, watching me, laughing to herself, sort of, obviously feeling seedy. And this did not make yours truly feel easy, for by this time I was in a more scholarly frame of mind and wished to pursue my functional anthropologist leanings rather than . . . Well, you know. So I pretended to ignore her.

But she wasn't buying that. She jumped up, tore into her bedroom and returned with a stack of eight-by-ten photographs of herself, for gosh sakes, in all sorts of lewd poses.

Well, believe me, those pictures were sickening. I mean! I won't, for gosh sakes, go into detail. That would be extremely unprintable as well as immoral and illegal.

All I could think of, as I thumbed through them (still going along with my when-in-Rome approach) —all I could think of was the time Dad published in our hometown newspaper his sheer genius of an appeal to fathers of teenage daughters. (The wire services weren't on the ball, as usual, so they didn't pick it up for worldwide distribution.) But in it, Dad warned all fathers to be on guard against (and he coined the following phrase) insipient moral decay provoked by trash which still passes for respected periodic organs. Then, in the body of his thesis, he proved it. Dad, needless to say, is a brilliant writer. Simply fabulous. Probably the jerks who work for the wire services were too stupid to know what he was talking about, being too stupid to read brilliant writing. Dad always says that they (journalists) constantly reveal their stupidity, not only in their own writings,

but also in *what* they choose to write *about*. Most of
the time, I mean. Of course, there are good and bad
in every profession, and some who turn bad can be
straightened out, sometimes. Like our editor, Mort
Copton. Mort once printed the picture of some Hollywood movie star (scantily clad) right on Page One.
That was when he first came to our town. He knows
better now. Dad and the board got him on the carpet
and kept him there for over an hour about that lewd
picture, and he's behaved himself ever since.

But—yet again like a clever cigarette advertisement—I digress.

It became quite clear to me, as I gave the matter
some more hard, bold, analytical thought, that I was
going to find myself out—O-U-T out! If I didn't
comply with my keeper's brazenly revealed wishes.
(I say *revealed* because she just lay there watching
me.) (I mean, watching and *smiling*. The whole time
I thumbed through those sickening photos.) (And it
was obvious what was on her mind.) (And also that
I had to, as they say, take care of her or I'd be O-U-T.)

So I did.

After a delay, during which (and I refuse, as usual,
to go into the lurid details) she attempted to belittle
my manhood, for one thing. To egg me on, I suspect.
That seemed to be the only reason for some of the
smirking things she said. (I mean I'm rather well
endowed, physically as well as intellectually, and she
tried to poke fun at me, sort of. Belittle me, like. Trying to make me assert myself is the only reason I could
find for her doing such a thing, because as it turned
out, she didn't mean it.)

What followed is, of course, unmentionable, though

I might sum it up in general terms, in keeping with the standards I've established, and say simply that I did indeed make her say Uncle. I mean, I left no doubts in her mind as to my chesty manhood and virility.

Enough said.

Except that I should also add, parenthetically, (I went back to thinking in representations, as I previously pointed out that I sometimes do. I thought : I will be a representation of the entire white race and show this little colored girl, paid and professional though she is, that this business Hank keeps handing me about non-whites being sexually superior is . . . Bird Feed !)

I mean, don't get me wrong. I'm not, for gosh sakes, prejudiced ! On the other hand, I'm no idiotic Negrophile like Hank and some of those jerks. Besides, she was only sixteen years old. Or, so she told me, and I'm sure she couldn't have been much older than I, so if she jipped by a couple of years, what difference. The point is, she was young. So I figured now was the time to strike—to impress her, to let her know just how a real he-man goes about things, because the way she acted, she'd known nothing but (to use a word Hemingway has used) pansies. Which left me with one huge lurking fear : That I might have succeeded too well. After all, not every guy can make a paid professional lady of ill repute say Uncle.

(Though I will, before closing this chapter, say I did make a few concessions and go to some unplanned tactics in order to achieve this feat.)

Here goes me, I doosh out. Nex thing I find, Jimmyboy lookin at tee vee. Yeah, he sittin on the floor lookin an lissenin.

I say, Gee-zuz, Jimmy! I say, What the hell you gonna do now? You gonna jes sit an look at that mothahflippin glassface?

He say, Yeah.

I say, Ain nothin on tee vee. I say, Ain never nothin on tee vee sep the man puttin numbers on the map, an he ain on jes now. Turn that glassface bastid off! You hear?

He say, News comin on. He say, News an then this here other show comin on. He say, He wanna see this other show.

I say, Piss! I say, Sweet Jimmy Baby don't watch that crap. It make you nuts! It make you nutty's if you was livin down souff.

But he ain lissenin t'me. He lookin at ol glassface. She-it!

Tee vee say, News.

I can' see nothin new bout the news. They show Merican flag an Navy boats an airplanes an bombs blowin up, an all like that.

Ain nothin new bout that !

Then this tee vee Whiteman come on an he start talkin. Gee-zuz he talkin !

He stop talkin, some Whitechick come on an she singin. She singin bout beer. She jes wrinkle up her face an singin like she got her some longgone boyfrien' made o'beer an her lil ol pussy jes a-creamin fer her beer boyfrien'. Then this other tee vee Whiteman come on an he say, Syen-tifick ree-serch perfeck this beer this here Whitechick creamin her pussy bout.

What the hell this syen-tifick ree-serch big-word noise he talkin? Ooh-wee !

Firs' tee vee man come back an he start in talkin agen, an this time he talkin like he all fuss up. Yeah ! He talkin up an he talkin down, he talkin eas' and he talkin wes'. One time, he soun hurt. Nex, he soun happy. He go, like, Wee diddledee dee dee ! Then he go, Mumble mumble mumble !

She-it.

He talkin, pitchers come on, show some Niggerman gittin shoved roun by some Whitemen.

Ain nothin new bout that neither.

Nex come on pitchers show some poor Whitetrash man, tee vee man say they is gonna *kill* him. He say this poor ol Whitetrash done been foun *sane* ! Like, he ain no flip, he's okay in the head so they is gonna kill him in the lectrick chair !

Yeah ! He say that ! Right out loud he say that !

Kee-ryess ! They alla time killin somebody, them Whitefolks on tee vee. They shootin an fightin an playin lawman, an they killin an killin.

Make me sick ! No dam wonner I gotta show my Jimmyboy pitchers an give him teechin fore he kin play pritty, he so fulla fightin an killin. Like in the cathouse, he mix up fightin wiff funnin. This mothahless tee vee! Gee-zuz! Sometime I is gonna go on that tee vee an show them dum Whitefolks. I is gonna put on a cathouse show, same time they is puttin on them dum killin shows. Yeah! Hee hee!

Nother tee vee Whiteman come on, he say, Advertizin is how come Mericans livin a *good* life!

Yeah! No crap! He say that!

He say, Advertizin, an he say, Good Merican life!

He say *that*, I know them Whitefolks all so fuggin bigword nutty they is like one big fruitcake!

Then this firs' tee vee man come back, an he say, Ike flew off somewhere, an then more pitchers come on, show a lotta hiyella folks yellin *They Likes Ike*!

Yeah! Gee-zuz! How come them dum mothahs yellin like that? Why she-it, they don' even know Ike! Firs' time they ever even *seen* Ike! Can' even talk Inglish, yellin *They* likes *Ike*!

Phew!

Nex, they showin some rockit an tee vee man talkin up a mothahfuggin storm! Alla roun this rockit, Whitemen is jes a runnin an runnin, an they is more standin an sittin in rooms, an pushin this an pushin that, an everythin so spooky, an everybody so all fuss up. Then comes some weird noises jes like in a spook movie, all kinda weird noises like hootin an buzzin an boomin an hissin an Gee-zuz! Alla time tee vee man keep talkin like he bout t'flip. He jes git t'talkin so fast, I can' find out what the fug everybody so flip-floppin crazy over.

Nex, this rockit, he go *zoom*! Real big, he go, like, ZOOM! An he hiss an he puff an he start goin up.

Yeah! Like he start slow, and then Gee-zuz! He go like somebody stick a firecracker up his asshole. Great big mothahless rockit go up, an up, an up, an Kee-ryess!

Then all them spook noises stop an they all stop runnin an talkin, an everybody jes lissen t'his hissin. Then they gits all fuss up agen, on'y this time, they starts pattin each other on they backs, an yellin an wavin arms, an like that.

She-it! Them Whitefolks so dum! So screwed up Skinny Minnie dum dum dum! They git more happy bout some dum rockit rackit than they does bout anythin else. They make my poor ol blackass Pickaninny me jes ache! They likes Ike, and they likes rockits. They shoots rockits up, an they shoots each others dead.

News done, I is tellin Jimmy how dum them Whitefolks is, an he is tellin me, Shut up!

Yeah! He say he wanna see this other show. He tell me shut up an then he go git him a chair an he set in a chair steada on the nice soff floor wiff some pillas. Gee-zuz! But he look so godam funny sittin there, I can' help laughin.

I laugh, he say Shhh!

She-it!

Nex, this whole big buncha tee vee Whitemen come on. Sep, these ones, they got them one Niggerman wiff them. They say, He is from Africa. Yeah! He's from Africa is what they say.

He smile like a cottinpicker, seem t'me. Yeah, he smile cottinpickin kissass. Anyhow, he's all dress up o'fay.

They all sittin roun some ol table an lookin an talkin like somebody dyin. They jes a-sittin roun talkin sad. They talkin bout Russians an rockits an like that.

One Whiteman, he say them Russians gonna blow everybody up wiff they rockits an bombs like they got.

How come they wanna do that? I can' unnerstan that crazy-ass crap. Sep down souff. Some souff White-folks wanna kill every nigger livin, seem like, but that ain the same. Them souff Whitefolks, they is *way* gone! They is so far nuts, they ain never comin back, Ain the same's them Russianfolks, seem t'me. I don' know nothin bout them, sep they got them mothahless rockits an now these White mothahs say they wanna blow everybody up.

Tha's what they say! But alla time they sayin this, they is talkin bout blowin them Russianfolks up!

Phew!

Oncet, I dream I'm workin an in come a whole buncha Russian tricks. I go on upstairs wiff one an he pull down his pants an he ain got no cock a-tall! No! Stead, what he got, he got him a rockit. Yeah! He got him a rockitcock steada mancock! I say, Gee-zuz Russianman, how m'I gonna do my stuff wiff a rockit-cock? But he jes a-talkin like a tee vee Whiteman an I can' unnerstan a word he is sayin. I say t'myseff— I dreamin this—I say, Russianman, what the hell m'I gonna do wiff a rockitcock?

I bout t'tell Jimmy my dream, but I kin see he ain fer lissenin t'me. His ol eyeballs jes like they froze on that mothahfuggin glassface bastid. Them sad ol tee vee men, they still talkin Russians an rockits an all kinda big-word noise like that. This one trick, he keep sayin, Na'shall defense, na'shall defense. He wearin him a soljer suit. He all fuss up. He talk like he from down souff. He talk like a Koo Klux Klan man, an like he ain got him no mancock neither. Yeah, he talk like he got him a knifecock. Some o'them souff Whitefolks, all they wanna do is talk nasty an ack mean. Specially t'Niggers. This mothah, he sure wanna ack mean, but I ain sure *who* he wanna ack mean *to* !

She-it ! Me, I jes a simple-ass lil ol Pickaninny cat, I can' unnerstan why them Whitefolks git all fuss up an ack so mean an make everythin so all mix up wiff nucler bombs an shootin an all that crap. Jimmy, he bein White, maybe he unnerstan what they is doin. He ack like he do.

I say t'myseff, I say, Girl now you got you a sweet Whiteboy loverman, maybe he kin teach you bout what all them tee vee mothahs tryin t'do, an how come the Russianfolks an them Whitefolks wanna blow each others up.

I say, Jimmy?

He say, Shhh !

I say, *Hey* Jimmy ! I say, What're them crazy fay son-a-bitches up to, anyhow?

He say, Shhh !

Yeah ! All he gonna say, Shhh, shhh, shhh !

She-it ! What I say, I say, she-it !

I'm gonna throw that mothahfuggin tee vee out. I can' unnerstan it and it can' unnerstan me. An all Jimmy gonna do is say Shhh-shhh ! Yeah ! Nex chance I git, I'm gonna kick livin hell outta that tee vee an throw his dum ass right out. Soon's Jimmy done lookin his glassface in the eye, out he goes ! The tee vee.

On'y reason I come by his ol noisy glassface is cause-a Dolly. She the cat live in this partmin fore me. She an Madam buy all this stuff tha's here now, tee vee an all. Then she up an move on outta here. Yeah! She git herseff a Big Big Money Honey from Miami an go off wiff him. Lucky Dolly. She hiyella. She leave my blackass Pickaninny me a nice place, sep fer that tee vee.

On'y thing I kin ever watch is when this Whiteman in the mornin put the numbers on the map. Yeah! Everythin else a buncha crap. This man, he writin an he sayin, real real nice an smooth, he sayin, Dallas ... Forty, thirty-two. An he sayin, Denver ... Forty, thirty-*one*! Like, thirty-ONE, is how he says it. Sep, he say it real real soff, like, Da-ay-al-as, an like, Den-n-n-n-ver. Way he say it, soun so pritty. An when he says a number, tha's the very fuggin number he writes. Yeah! No perten, no crap! He writes jes what he is sayin.

But he's the on'y one that glassface ever come on wiff that do things nice an smooth an pritty an right. Course, they got some comics on tee vee advertizin, an they make me laugh a lil, but I don' like the way they is alla time tryin fer my pocketbook. So I kin dam well do wiffout the comics. Worff it t'git that other noise the fug outta here.

Yeah! Nex time Jimmy ain lookin, I is gonna toss that mothahless glassface clean outta here. Yeah! I ain gonna let it drive me jittery like it drive some folks, Black and White. I is gonna git me a stick an beat the crazy-ass na'shall defense outta it, an I is gonna do this in *seff* defense!

Yeah!

Sep, meantime, Jimmy still lookin like his eyeballs

froze. An this other tee vee mothah is sayin he hopes everybody in'ested in what he is sayin. Gee-zuz! He say it like if you ain in'ested, you ain worff she-it, way he say it. Then he goes off wiff more o'his big-word noise agen, an Jimmy he gittin all fuss up at this tee vee man talkin. I kin tell, way he lean over.

I say—real loud—I say, Jimmy yer *nuts*! Yeah! You let that dee-fuggin-dum noise git you, yer nuts!

He look mad an wave his hand fer me t'shut up. Kee-ryess!

Then, bout this time, I git saved by naecher. Yeah, I feel me a big wind comin on. I say t'myseff, Girl here goes yer chance! Yeah!

I git up an go right up t'that glassface bastid an I swing ass roun sos's I'm spades ace t'his glassface an I fart! Yeah! Man I let go real long an loud!

But Gee-zuz! Soon's I fart, tee vee start more o'his hissin an hottin an boomin, an Kee-ryess! I like t'pop clean outta my black hide! I turn roun an here goes this other fuggin rockit, up up up.

An right now, Jimmy, he stan up too, an he start in rantin an ravin.

I'm fartin, tee vee's hissin, Jimmy's rantin and ravin!

Ooh-wee! I can' tell which he is most mad at, me or the tee vee, so I let go one more. Jes because!

Then Jimmy git his jaws a-puffin an a-goin somethin awful! He wavin his hands an he walkin back an forff, an he lookin like he is gonna crap! Yeah! He look like he is gonna crap right now. On my nice rug!

He tellin me I don' know wha's goin on in the worl'.

I say, Piss on the worl'. I know wha's goin on right here.

He wanna know, Don' I even care bout Wes' Berlin?

I tell him he kin shove Wes' Berlin up his ass an go t'the moon fer all I care.

He say, Ain I Merican? He say, Is I Kalmnist? Or is I Apeezer?

He talkin like that, an he talkin freedom an Merican way an he talkin all that semi-demi big-word noise we jes been hearin on tee vee. Gee-zuz! He wrinkle up his face an jes talk an talk like them mothahless tee vee table men.

I say, Merican? Kalmnist? Apeezer? I say, Jimmy is you *blind*? Can' you see I is jes a lil ol blackass Picka- ninny cat?

He say, My color got nothin t'do wiff it. Ab-slootly nothin!

Yeah! He say that. Kee-ryess! He so fur out dum!

I say, Jimmy you kiss my blackass, you don' like the way I do roun here. This *my* place. Madam pays the rent here so's I kin live here steada wiff them older cats. This ain yer place. It's mine, man! You don' like it, you kin jes drop gelt an git. Go on, feed this kitty an shoo! An you kin take ol glassface wiff you. Boff o'you dum daddios kin jes git the hell outta here.

Nex, he wrinkle up sorta dum an he quit talkin so godam loud. But he still jes a-puffin an blowin and I can' unnerstan what he bout t'toot out now, sep I know he ain been lissenin t'my talkin cause he is talkin way far off from jack. He is talkin so far from payin up, he is makin me jittery. He ain talkin payin, an he ain talkin goin, an he ain talkin comin back.

I say t'myseff, Girl you is jes plain losin yer invessment! This madass Big Money Honey ain talkin like no invessment no more. He's talkin like some tee vee terrible. He Merican this an Merican that, an he Kalmnist this an Kalmnist that, but he way far off from jack!

I say, Jimmy shut the fug up. I say, Jimmy fore you go, I wanna hunner. Yeah, Jackie say weekend is one hunner, an if the trick don' stay all weekend, tough shitski, it still cost him one hunner.

He say, Whaaa?

I say, Hunner, tha's *whaaa*! One big ol green-ass hunner!

He say, Crissmiss crissmiss crissmiss! He say, He can' unnerstan what I'm talkin bout.

I say, Like hell you can' unnerstan! You godam well can so unnerstan. I'm talkin jack, man! I'm talkin bout *yer* jack! I'm talkin that great big wingdingin wad you got in yer pants. I say, Man you got some weekend pussy, now I want me my bread. I want my jack jack jack!

Nex, I gotta do some fancy dancin fore I git me my hunner.

Now I'm no stupe. I mean, even if I *am* flunking those three subjects—biology, psychology, French— heck! I could have passed those midterms if I'd memorized properly, and—no question about it—I'll make it up during the second half semester. Because when I feel like it, I can get plenty intellectual. Not that I'm an out and out egghead, understand, but I do like a good intellectual TV show once in awhile. I mean, I have a distinct bent in that direction. You know, like the CBS specials and the Huntley-Brinkley sort of thing. So, after she'd said Uncle for me, I tuned in on this highbrow show. Very important. About national defense.

It had been mentioned in class and I'd seen it advertised in the paper. (Though, to be perfectly honest, I thought the ad called it a foreign affairs program instead of a national defense one.) (But what's the difference.) The point is, I knew it was important for college guys like I, who will be leaders of the entire Free world one of these days.

Also, I know old Prof. Wilbur would be asking questions about it Monday morning because he's all gung-ho about current events and I'm passing political science and want to keep passing. And, having obliged my colored 'keeper' (ha ha), I figured she'd leave me alone for awhile. But, of course, you never can tell when girls like her will get another case of . . . I'll call it *excitement*, and want to drag a guy back down on the floor again. So, also, I figured I'd better take this opportunity to rest up, if you get what I mean. By this time, I was beginning to get afraid she was falling in love with me, and that would be bad. I mean! After all, I had showed her a trick or two, so to speak, even if she was a professional—with my representative thinking proving very very satisfying.

(Although, however, a week or so later, I remembered my original slave-to-employee representative thinking, like I was thinking while in the ill repute house. I cringe to think what certain unorthodox elements of my conduct during the latest indecent time in her apartment would add to *that*. I mean, like, slavery, emancipation, and ? ? ?) (However, we won't go into that.)

But—to get back to this highbrow show—(which incidentally, led to an unexpected event) I was sitting in one of her very modern chairs, just sitting there (nude), watching TV. First the news and then this highbrow show. Now, in order for you to fully appreciate what happened later, I must tell you about this program. Detail it as a unit, so to speak.

Primarily, it was a bi-partisan discussion of the world arena and our relative strength, with yardsticks for measuring same. That is, our deterent capabilities and military posture, including secret shortterm and secret longterm plans past the drawing-board stage, already operational, almost, and also what the communists have. I mean, it was a penetrating search to define clearly Russian aggression in all its broader aspects, with due regard for communism's more subtle and insidious cancerous threats to the West, including comparative propaganda advantages in the space race—touching, as it went, on such staggering problems as the status of West Berlin and economic breakthroughs to underdeveloped peoples in the Poverty Belt, including the crying need for taxpayers to tighten their belts and get behind Freedom's Fiscal Policy, and above all the threat to our nation's security posed by various total disarmament plans, and the possibilities for further negotiations along this line.

Well, right off the bat, this one commentator starts in talking like America is done for, for gosh sakes! (It's one of those unrehearsed shows, which are the best kind, since nothing is planned.) And this guy is going on about anti-missile-missiles and anti-anti-missile-missiles, and becoming quite intellectual and scientific. (Which I like. I mean, when they get real highbrow. A guy gets tired of nothing but westerns and detective stories.) But what I don't like is some joker talking as if the Russians could blow us off the *map*! I don't know just who this one commentator thought he was, but it's a good thing there were those other guys—congressmen and military persons, mostly with one rep from an underdeveloped and newly emerging African nation which has recently achieved Freedom and is now cementing its achievement. Well, these guys let the jerk prattle on about how he thought the Russians were *advanced,* for gosh sakes, in missiles.

(I mean, the way he talked, you'd get the impression that even SAC was no match for Russian rocketry, for crying out loud!)

Then this one general comes on strong. I mean, he lets this jerk have it. The general asks, 'How do you know how many missiles the Russians have, or how good their missiles are?'

Ha!

That showed that dirty parlor pink. He was pretty quiet after that. Which gave the military persons and congressmen a chance to get down to brass tacks. They proved with hard cold facts that America has an adequate military posture, counting SAC, and is all set to blast those dirty communists if they so much as look cockeyed. (They didn't say it in those words, understand, but they made themselves plain. I got the message okay, and was proud to be an American.)

And, as for the other urgent issues pressing this country, the military persons pointed to the crux of the problem—which I remembered and mentioned in Pol. Sc. class Monday—which is *money*! The government simply needs more tax money to maintain our military posture and facilitate longrange plans already past the drawing-board stage and operational almost, but not yet on the assembly line, and it's the lack of money which is the holdup.

(It's hard to imagine what these new secret weapons are, but it's fun to try.)

But before we got to the end of the program—which was to be a debate between this dirty pink jerk who thought we should scrap the H bomb, for crying out loud, and an Air Force person who was going to *attempt* to tell this appeaser the obvious A-B-C's of

why we don't—my colored girl started behaving like a
wild woman. I mean, she had been nervous and fidg-
etty all along, but I figured that was because she was
just spoiled and wanted me to pay constant attention
to *her*. Of course, I excused her behavior then,
because . . . Well, after all, she was unintelligent and
uneducated, but—

All of a sudden she walks up to the TV screen,
turns an about-face, bends over with her rear facing
the set and—

Passed air !

Can you imagine such a thing !

She did this just as they were presenting the count-
down for the launching of an Atlas, and when they
launched it, she jumped like they had launched *her* !

Which served her right. I mean, I didn't mind her
clowning around so much, as long as she didn't get
between the set and me, or get disgusting and start
passing air—but when she did *that*, I gave her heck !

After all, what kind of an American would not only
ignore these gravely important matters, but act like
she did to boot? I mean, even if she was an underworld character. After all !

Well, I told her. I told her that as a Freedom-
loving citizen of this great nation, she had no right,
no right whatsoever, absolutely no right in the world
to behave in such a way toward people who are working night and day to save the world for the American Way and keep her safe from communistic dictatorship. (Though, later, I got to thinking again, and
I thought : Maybe, JC, you shouldn't have scolded
her quite so much, because she was unintelligent and
uneducated and also underworld, so how could she

know about the horrors of Marxism. After all, it's up to persons like you, JC, college guys who will carry these burdensome problems, to look out for people like her, who have low mentality and corrupt morals.) (I mean, tolerance! That's what's needed!)

But at the time, I did give her What-For. I told her she'd best watch the way she acted about things like this nation's security, and I tried to explain how important such matters are, but she just stood there, half-clowning, half-sarcastic, and kept between me and the TV, all the time jabbering this awful profanity of hers and making it absolutely clear that she didn't care at all—for West Berlin, even!

Some people! They're hopeless, some people are. I thought: Sister, if you're going to behave like this, I'll leave. I'll just relinquish my scientific and functional anthropological approach and leave. And I told her I would.

Well! She thereupon flew into this terrible rage, jumping up and down, shouting, 'Jack!' and I don't know what all. She used so much profanity, it was difficult to catch whatever it was she was trying to tell me. But one thing loomed as evident: she was becoming unreasonable. Even threatening.

So I—right then and there—decided I'd better scram. (She had mentioned something about my getting out during that obscene tirade she went through; I caught that much.) So I went for the bedroom to get my clothes.

And then it started! Christmas! Then it really actually started!

Dear Reader, get this picture: One minute, she's a quiet little dark brown buffoon (nude), running around, acting nervous, but not serious. Sort of comic, if you get what I mean. And then, the very next instant, she's rushing around like she lost her mind, and when I went toward the bedroom, she flew over like she'd been shot from a cannon! She buzzed right on ahead of me and stationed herself in the bedroom doorway, and stood there blocking my path, snarling and sneering and pointing her fingernails at me. Like an insane animal, I swear!

Well, she sneered and snarled and let loose with this long jabber of profanity for awhile, and I stood frozen in my tracks. I just let her jabber on. I didn't move a muscle. I was too surprised.

Then, just as quickly, she sort of wound down. I mean, it was as if she'd run out of breath. She gave a sort of half-sob, took a deep breath, sighed and then —Bamb! She just slumped down to the floor and let go this big long moan.

Well, I certainly took advantage of that opportunity, I can tell you. Yes sir, I missed not one second. I rushed on and leaped over her and into the bedroom I went. I grabbed my shorts and tee shirt and socks, and started putting them on as fast as I could.

But I wasn't fast enough.

All the time I'm trying to get into my clothes, I can hear her yelling, in some other part of the apartment. I can't catch it all, but I can hear her yell, 'Jack, Jack, Jack!' (And at this juncture, I thought Jack was probably some gangster or thug who lived next door to her and would come barging in any second now, beat me up and take my money, maybe.) (Which surmise proved erroneous.)

Because the next thing I knew, in she rushed like a half-back on a touchdown run, carrying this huge kitchen knife.

Well, by this time she was completely out of her stupid mind. I mean, she was acting like an insane female Errol Flynn (colored) in one of those old fashioned movies where they have swords and go at each other like mad. I mean, there I was in the process of pulling on my shorts (she was that quick) and there she was, in dueling position, waving that kitchen knife at my private parts. I thought : Christmas, JC! The next thing you know you'll be castrated!

But I had little time for the thinking process. I mean we went round and round that room, she chasing me, of course, with that knife and me trying to get into my shorts and keep away from her at the same time, and not being exactly entirely successful in either endeavor.

And—what do you know! The very next instant, she wasn't chasing me any more. She had hauled my trousers out of her closet and was off like a shot for the livingroom again.

So, by this time, of course, it dawned on me : She wants my money! That's it! That's what all this is about. Money! All along, what she's been going wild about is money.

And that, as you can undoubtedly well imagine, Dear Reader, came as quite a severe shock. I mean, after all, how the heck should I have known? She had acted as if money were the furthest thing from her stupid mind. She never even so much as mentioned the A-B-C of M-O-N-E-Y, money! Not since I'd given her that $10 back at the ill repute house, I mean. Besides, she'd gone so far as to give me the key to her apartment!

I was forced to conclude that she was so immoral she didn't care if I was a fellow underworld character and in trouble with the police. If I had one red cent, she was going to steal it!

Anyway, now that she had it, she had stopped zooming around like she was about to chop me up or climb walls, or something. I peeked into the living-room and there she was, sitting in the middle of the floor (sort of squatting on her haunches) holding the knife in one hand and my trousers in the other, looking like a cowering animal. She just sat there for a time, staring at yours truly and mumbling some more of her profane jabberings and waving that knife back and forth, and shaking my trousers occassionally.

I thought: Well, James Cartwright Holland, no use endangering your very life by resisting a crazed stickup artist. Let her take the money. I mean, it's plain to see she is armed and dangerous. Not to mention unstable.

So I finished dressing, then came out to the living-room, and there she sat, still, but now she had my money in a pile by her side—a pile upon which rested her weapon.

I approached with caution. Both of us were silent. It was a tense moment. (I mean, I couldn't leave without my trousers.) (If she took it into her head to add one more crime to her growing list and destroy my trousers, I'd be in a difficult position indeed!)

But she didn't. She stared at me sullenly for a moment, then tossed my trousers at me. And, as I climbed into them, she lowered her eyes in guilty shame. (Or, so it seemed at the time, though I was later to learn she was incapable of any such noble emotion.)

And me? I thought : JC my boy, this is no place for a whiteman. And forthwith—stopping only long enough to grab my shoes in the foyer—was on my way out, when—Bamb!

Nᴇx, Gee-zuz! Here goes Jimmy out the door. Yeah!

I say t'myseff, I say, Whoa! This ain gonna do no good. No good a-tall. There goes my invessment an all my cottinpickin considerin.

I hide my jack unner the divan fast's I kin, an I up an on my runnin way. Time he git t'the door, I git t'him, an then—

Kee-ryess! He opens the door an guess who's there. Francine!

Yeah! I bout squat. Right now!

She say, Ooh! She say, Hee!

I say, Kee-ryess!

She say, She hear this terrible rackit downstairs, she come runnin t'see wha's-a trouble.

I say, Trouble? Ain no trouble till you come, Francine. I say, So how bout you jes go right back, huh?

But she push right on in. Jes take my Jimmy the cheatin burgler by the arm an wiggleworm along. Then she takes off her shoes an sets 'em down like she gonna stay a week.

She say, Kitten I don' know you got this boy down here. Who's he?

I say, None o'yer dam bizness, Francine.

She say, Aaah Kitten, that ain no way t'talk. She say, Seem like I seen this boy someplace. She say, Hee hee!

Then she see my blade. Yeah!

See, I gotta fetch me this blade counta Jimmy bein so rump-thumpin knuckleheaded dum. He fixin t'run off without payin up, is how come. Yeah! I git me this blade an swing roun some t'help make him unnerstan. Tha's when I gotta do me all that ooh-wee godam fancy dancin. T'make him unnerstan.

Francine, she see this blade, she say, Hey Kitten, wha's this fer?

An I jes shut ass right up tight.

An Francine, she jes keep a-comin an a-hangin on Jimmy. She don' know which end up, but she tryin awful hard t'find out.

Jimmy, he don' know which end up neither. He ack like he wanna go an he wanna stay, like he don' know what the hell he wanna do. He lookin at me an lookin at Francine, an lookin at me agen.

I figure no use makin Francine all fuss up. I say t'myseff, Keep cool, Kitten, an that ass-sniffin son-a-bitch take off pritty soon. Francine.

But she gotta bad ol look in her eye, like she is fixin t'have Kitten fer dinner. An bout right now, *I* dam well don' know which fuggin end is up neither. Too!

She say, Hey Kitten, I gotta idea.

I say, Take yer idea an shove it, Francine.

She say, Ah Kitten. She say, Now be nice, Kitten. She say, Maybe this nice Whiteboy wanna see him a show. Huh?

I say, No Francine, he don' wanna see no show.

But she keep comin affer me anyhow. Yeah! She let go Jimmy an she affer my ass.

I say, Git away, you crabass! I tol' you, he don' wanna see him no show. You jes git outta here an leave us be.

But she keeps houndin me. I'm movin roun the room tryin t'git away an she's movin roun affer me. I move slow, she move slow. I move fast, she move fast.

She-it!

This fuggin Francine, she been sniffin roun me since Madam find me by the police house when I was jes a lil tiny Pickaninny. An now she ack like she gonna git me. Kee-ryess!

She jes crazy the way she wanna do. Same time it make me wanna laugh. Jimmy standin there watchin us, make me wanna laugh too. He standin there wiff his jaw hangin down an his eyeballs poppin out. I can' help it, I git t'laughin.

Nex, I fall down. Yeah! Movin roun like that an laughin I miss a step an—plop! Down I go, wiff that godam Francine down right on top, an alla time I'm laughin up a bellyache.

I'm laughin till I see that godam Francine is eye level wiff my hunner. Yeah! She look right, she gonna see my hunner unner the divan. She see my loot, I'm really in trouble.

Right now, I wiggle out an git away an git up an run. Yeah! I run right fer the phone.

An I say, Francine I tol' you t'git. Now git!

But she still jes keep a-comin. She lookin at me an she lookin at Jimmy an she smilin real kissass.

She say, I got some gen'lemen frien's upstairs, an they is lovers. How bout if—

Ooh-ooh-ooh Skinny Minnie.

She goes on, sayin why don' me an Jimmy come on upstairs wiff her an see her crazy-ass frien's, an like that. Alla time she is talkin she is tryin t'git at my bizness.

An Jimmy, he git his face all wrinkle up, she talkin an messin like that.

Kee-ryess!

I say, Francine you ain rollin outta here time I count t'three, I'm gonna phone.

An I lay my hand on that phone an I start in countin.

One ... two ...

An she say, No no no Kitten.

An I say, Yeah! I say, You ain on yer way right now, I'm gonna phone fer Jackie!

She go. Yeah! I say, real loud an mean, I say, *Phone fer Jackie,* and she outta my partmin that fast.

Ooh-wee! Gee-zuz!

Sep, my troubles ain over yet. No-oh-oh! Jimmy still lookin nothin but all fuggin up in the air. He walkin back an forff, an he wrinkle up one minit, an he snort the next. He look at me an he start in rattlin off, an then he go back t'walkin an lookin agen.

I say, Jimmy Baby don' pay no mind t'Francine.

But he jes do him some more o'his dum rantin an ravin an big-word noise.

So I shut up. I say t'myseff, Girl at least he ain gone. Tha's the big thing, he ain gone. Francine done save yer invessment, yer very first invessment. Stumble-ass is how, but she done it anyhow. An now she is gone an he is here, so back t'work.

I say—sweet's I kin—I say, Jimmy Honey take a seat an cool it. I say, How you like it I go an put on some nice swingin music, real sad an pritty.

But he jes say, like, Mumble mumble mumble. Like a godam tee vee man, but he sit down, talkin like that. So I put on some nice soff tinklin swingin stuff.

I say t'myseff, Girl you got yer one hunner fer the weekend now, you can' let him go out that door mad. He do that, he ain never comin back, an you ain got you no cottinpickin chance fer yer first invess-ment nohow!

Again I wish I were a paid professional writer so I could describe it to you. What happened when I went to leave, I mean. Because the whole thing was like a stag party and I don't know how I could tell it without impairing the high standards of this account. I mean, I don't know how I could get around the indelicacy of it and still indicate how comical it was.

Now don't get me wrong. I was sickened. In fact, I was horrified! And I wouldn't have laughed at all if it hadn't seemed so much like a dream—the sort of nightmare one might have after having eaten ice-cream just before bedtime.

But how can I present a true and accurate factual picture? (Truth is stranger than fiction!) (I mean, you can't *imagine*!)

What I'm driving at is . . . Well, let me tell just enough, as Prof. McGillicuty says. (About literature, that is. *Great* literature, I mean. He says the author must tell as much as he can, as concisely as he can, in a few well-chosen words, and above all, without becoming indecent and using four-letter words.) (He says literature has its laws and principles too, of course, which makes science not the *only* thing!)

(And the big literary law is to avoid obscenities.) So let me try, in a few well-chosen words, to tell what happened.

Which, believe me, such an endeavor is, in this case, very much uneasy. What I mean is, right off the bat, I don't know for certain if Kitten ran after me before I opened the door, or at that very instant, or maybe it was a moment later. The point is: She ran. She zoomed up behind me all of a sudden, cooing like a little pigeon again.

(Unbelieveable! She could coo like a pigeon one moment and scream like a banshee the next, and go right back to coo-ing again, as if such quick changes were the most natural thing in the world!)

Anyhow, when I opened the door, who should I find myself face to face with?

That other paid professional prostitute—the same one who kept running in and out of our room in the ill repute house!

Holy Christmas! I mean! Here's the picture, Dear Reader: I'm standing there, dressed, with my shoes in my hand, and behind me is Kitten, nude, tugging at my coattail, and in front of me is this Francey (though I'm certainly well aware of the fact that that was probably not her real legal name but an assumed name for professional purposes) and she is dressed up fit to kill in this gaudy evening gown that is tight and has a very low neckline and is this pukey-looking green color, which in itself is enough to make a normal person's stomach turn.

So, of course, I couldn't go. I mean, she just stood there blocking the doorway, and I couldn't walk *through* her, for gosh sakes!

Then, immediately, the two of them began jabbering in their dialect and I didn't catch all they said. Francey spoke gently to Kitten, but Kitten literally scolded Francey and wanted her to leave. Which Francey didn't do. Instead, she took my arm and moved on into the apartment and spotted the knife Kitten had almost castrated me with.

And the next thing I knew, it started! Wow! I mean Francey (dressed) chased Kitten (undressed) all over the place until they both landed in a heap with Francey sort of climbing all over Kitten, like . . . Well, like I don't know what. I mean the whole thing seemed like a wild post-icecream dream, as mentioned above, or (I might as well say it) like a stag party movie. This Francey was literally making immoral passes at Kitten, and that, of course, was sickening. But what was comical was the way Kitten reacted. She kept trying to escape—dashing all over the floor, trying to get away from Francey, who came right after her, so that it became plain to any discerning eye that Francey was perverted, for crying out loud! I mean, she was sick sick sick!

Well, I froze in my tracks. I didn't know whether to throw up or laugh. I mean, our frat has this stag movie (which I, of course, have nothing to do with, no authority over at all) (so couldn't have it tossed out or burned, even if I wanted to) (which I do, of course)—and, anyway, this movie is the closest thing I've ever witnessed to what occurred at that time.

Then, to make things even more sickening, this Francey mentioned something about there being some homosexuals, even, upstairs in her apartment!

What a madhouse!

Fortunately, Kitten was able to escape by this time, and, giving her customary banshee yell, and shouting something about Jack again (but this time using the diminutive of Jack, namely, *Jacky*), and Francey took to her heels and ran out.

Then—the very next instant—Kitten was her soft coo-ing pigeon-like self again. Well, that was too much. I mean, I felt it was high time I tried to pound some morality into that girl, even if she was what she was. Not that what almost happened was her fault, because it wasn't. But she came out of it acting as calm and cool as you please—just like such mad insanity were an everyday occurrence. Which maybe it was, and that's worse. I mean, the girl had no *shame*! No shame whatsoever! So I made an attempt to enlighten her—to tell her about the awful danger, healthwise, both physically and mentally, which such behavior invariably leads to. What I mean is, I tried to explain the difference between normal marital sexual relations and abnormal perverted illegal immorality.

But, she was just too unintelligent and uneducated to grasp anything. She kept quiet and listened, all right, but I might have saved my breath, because when I'd finished this explanation (which I strenuously endeavored to make understandable to her level of mentality) she smiled her simple-minded smile, guided me to a chair and then trotted off to her bedroom to play her hi fi. I mean, I didn't expect her to immediately run off for some certified medical advice, or something, but neither did I expect her to indicate beyond a shadow of doubt that my efforts to enlighten her had been entirely and completely in vain.

Anyway, I sat. Matter of fact, I was too tired to do much of anything else. One minute she's got this knife and is chasing me around, trying to castrate me, and the next she's coo-ing like a love-sick pigeon, and in between she's clowning with a mental case. All of which is very tiring. I didn't know quite what to do, but since she insisted I stay, and also (above all) since she had stolen my money, I decided to hang around awhile longer, just to see what might develop.

Well, what developed was another wild row. I mean, no sooner had I seated myself comfortably and made myself at home when—Bamb!

Here's the picture: When she takes off for the bedroom, I switch on her TV—mainly because I was getting sick and tired of that stuff she called music. About the time she comes out of the bedroom and is on her way to the kitchen (to make us sandwiches, as it turned out) the TV warms up and comes on with this innocent and highly-rated western. *Matt Mellon*, as a matter of hard cold fact.

Then, like a bomb, she swung around and came hightailing it back with her fists clenched and this angry snarl on her lips, and stood there a moment, snarling at the TV image of Matt, played by . . . What's-his-name, the actor who's been married to the same wife for 15 years.

Then, Christmas! Fantastic as it may sound, she *attacked*! I mean literally attacked! The TV, that is. She rushed it—let out with her banshee yell and leaped at it, and grabbed it—wrapped her arms around it and (Unbelieveable!) lifted it off the floor —clear off the floor!

I thought for sure she was having a fit of some sort

and was about to run for my life. (Not that I'm
a coward, but like they say, when a person's out of his,
or her, mind, he or she has abnormal strength and,
above all, is unpredictable. And in view of how
unpredictable she'd been all along, and also when you
realize it was a 21-inch set she was lifting off the floor,
I was not for trusting to the shifting winds of fortune.)

However, right about here I realized what she was
trying to do, and so didn't run. She was (and I kid
thee not!) trying to throw her TV out the window!
The most comic part of this entire incident was: She
couldn't get the set to fit through the window. No
matter how she pushed and shoved and twisted, it
just wouldn't go. You see, the window, which was
this huge picture window which didn't open, had
two smaller windows on each side of it which did
open, and she had one of the side windows open and
was trying to get it through and toss it, for crying
out loud, out into mid air!

Imagine!

Please, Dear Reader, get the picture: We're four
stories up and there she is trying to heave that TV
out! Think of the mess it would have made when it
hit the sidewalk below. Christmas!

Which, fortunately for all and any concerned, it
didn't—but only because she couldn't get it out the
window. But, still jabbering her profanities, she laid
it on the floor face down, stood on the back of it,
grabbed the wire in both hands and gave one great
and horrendous tug. I mean, she pulled! She gave
this fierce grunt and heaved like a weightlifter in a
championship match. (For colored girls.) So naturally
the wire came out of the set. What else?

And when it did, she was caught off balance and almost landed on her head before she regained her balance again, still clutching that wire. Then she flopped back onto her couch and sat there, smiling this supercilious grin—just sat there like that.

Well! I mean! If only I were a paid professional writer and could describe how really insanely comic she looked standing (nude) on the back of that set, heaving with all her might and mane at that silly wire. I mean, if only I could do this scene justice. But that task, I fear, is beyond me.

Anyway, things sort of settled back down to a dull roar after that. She took off for the kitchen again and I was left with nothing but her idiotic music.

It was at this point that I reconnoitered. That is, I reached in my pocket and found she had left me some money : $10.45, for crying out loud !

I then made some quick calculations and realized I must have spent—on taxis, in that Black-n-Tan place, and at the ill repute house—about $16. Which, if deductive logic served me well, meant she had stolen about $100.

Well, a couple of things were involved here. For one thing, there was the principle of it—her stealing that money, even though she had been clearly informed that I was a fellow underworld character, proving again the old axiom : There's No Justice Among Thieves ! Another thing : Barbara and I had a date for Tuesday to go to the Playhouse and see a Shakespearean production which, counting dinner and drinks before, and a snack and more drinks later, would surely cost me at least $25, and maybe more. (You see, Barbara's father taught her to drink—as part of her preparation for college—and that's fine for her honor, of course. I mean, she sure can hold her liquor. On the other hand, her father did such a good job, she can toss down highballs with the best of them, and that gets expensive.) (Don't get me wrong. I'm happy to see her enjoying herself and don't begrudge the money it costs, and it's certainly heartening to find a girl who can drink large quantities without endangering her high morals.) However, the point I wish to stress is : $10.45 was not, for crying out loud, enough for a night at the Playhouse ! Not to mention such additional weekly details as cigarettes and coffee and lunches at the cafeteria until my next check arrived on Friday.

Obviously, further calculations were in order. I mean, what could Kitten have done with my money? Without a stitch on yet ! one minute she's sitting there in the middle of the floor holding it, and the next minute it's gone. Disappeared !

Well, my choice was clearcut. I mean, it was either leave now and let her steal my money—which would result in hardships Tuesday evening (to say the least) —or stay and, if possible, get it back.

Yes, it was a challange, and I couldn't resist it. Ha ha, thought I. This, James Cartwright Holland, is right up your alley. This will be fun.

Of course, right off the bat I realized I had to relinquish my scientific viewpoint towards this little experience and adopt a more pragmatic approach. But I didn't waste time with regrets about this. No !

Anxious to explore diplomatic channels first, I resorted immediately to the when-in-Rome frame of mind and got undressed again. That was the first step. I wasn't sure where I was going from there, but that was the very obvious first step.

And it wasn't long before my diplomatic approach paid off admirably. She, for gosh sakes, supplied yours truly with the very capital and position of strength my bargaining posture required.

Christmas! Like a bolt from the devine blue!

And, being quick-witted about such matters, I did indeed grab that capital position by its figurative wheel, so to speak, and steer fortune fore to aft, thus gaining the advantage—a slick maneuver which I will endeavor to recount in its proper place.

Kee-ryess! Firs' time my back is turn', that Fay
bastid Jimmy the mothahless burgler at that glassface son-a-bitch tee vee all over agen!

I swing ass back on in the livin room, big ol glassface makin a mos' terrible noise. He showin this
Whiteman shootin straight out! Yeah! He got him
two cowboy guns an he is jes a-shootin right square
in the face o'anybody dum enuff t'be lookin some
dum glassface in the eye.

Yeah! He do this!

An alla time he doin this shootin, this loud mothahless spook music go, like, Raie Raie Raie Raie! Like
t'rupture my ear!

Tween this boom boom Whiteman shootin, an this
raie raie noise music, that tee vee look like it gonna
blow up an kill everybody! Yeah! Boom boom! Raie
raie! Boom boom! Raie raie!

Gee-eee-eee-zuz! I can' take it! I jes can' take it
much longer. I *try*. Fer a minit.

On'y thing I kin tell is, this fuggin shootin Whiteman, he is good lookin an he is mean lookin, so's
everybody sposed t'know he perten t'be some six-

legged horse's ass of a cowboy lawman. He so crab-ass horsey mean lookin, he can' be nothin but a godam lawman!

Yeah!

I say t'myseff, I say, Girl it gonna be you, or it gonna be that mothahless madass boom boomin crap, one or the other.

Make me so jimjam jittery, I near nutty already. Fack, I jes ain even got no room leff in me fer Picka-ninny considerin. No room a-tall! No!

I grab that dum glassface. I grab that son-a-bitch an I pick his ass up an I carry him t'the winda, an I set him noise down, an I open the winda, and I pick his ass up agen, and I is gonna throw him right the hell outta my winda! Yeah! He is gonna hit an go boom oncet, an then he is gonna shut the fug up oncet an fer all!

Yeah!

Sep, on'y one thing wrong. He don' fit. I try, but nothin I do gonna make his noisey fat ass fit thru that lil winda. I do this an I do that. I up him down an back-ass him forwar', an still he don' fit.

An alla time I is doin this, that spiteful Whiteman pertenin t'be some cowboy lawman, an that raie raie still goin on, right in *my face!*

So I set his ass back down on the floor face down, an I grab him by his line. Yeah!

Gee-zuz! Ain nothin else I kin do t'kill that bastid, sep grab him by his lectrick line and pull it—*pop*! Right outta his ass!

Ooh-wee Skinny Minnie! That do it. Yeah, he is dead now. Yeah, an he ain gonna make no more fuggin rockit rackit now. No-oh-oh!

I do this, Jimmy jes sittin an lookin at me like I is
nuts. Humph! Kee-ryess! I kill that tee vee fer him
too! That glassface son-a-bitch, wiff all his shootin
and fightin an killin, like t'drive *him* nuts! Like t'drive
him nuts long ago, I spect.

I don' never like t'hurt nothin or nobody. No, not
never! But that everlastin boom boomin raie raie
crap, I gotta kill that son-a-bitch, I ain got no choice!
I don' kill *him*, he sure gonna same's kill *me*! An
even he don' never git t'killin me, he sure gonna make
my Whiteboy invessment nutter'n he already is.

So, tee vee is dead. Jimmy find he ain got no more
pocketpickin perten crap t'look at, he git up an take
off his dum clothes an he git cozy on my nice big rug,
an he lissen *at* my recordplayer.

Tha's better. Everythin better now. Wiff him cozy
an all paid up, an me wiff my hunner, an Francine
the hell outta here, an that everlastin boom boomin
raie raie done, at last everythin better.

Nice cool smooth sweet jazz tinklin, me makin us
sammages, steppin roun some, everythin better.

Phew!

Godam, I got news for Jackie! Invessment easy?
Ooh-wee! Considerin all the dancin an blade fetchin
I gotta do jes t'git my own weekend hunner, and
then that tee vee killin I gotta do t'keep my marbles,
an all that sadass big-word noise I gotta lissen to, I
bout ready t'figure maybe I oughtta wait'll I is fifteen
fore makin invessment.

Sep, maybe it gonna go okay now. Maybe he gonna
ack nice an git the right idea, an maybe we is gonna
git along jes fine. I hope he don' git him no more
dum ideas. I sure hope he don' cause he kin be okay.

When he wanna. Yeah! Oncet he been teeched, he do sweet an good playin turnabout, oncet he been teeched. He make me one fine invessment, he wanna.

Why Kee-ryess! All that fightin an teechin an killin done wiff now, maybe I find out I ain got me no lil ol pissy ant invessment. Maybe I find out I got me a whole flipfloppin fed'el budgit. Yeah! Hee hee!

Pritty cottinpickin nifty, too, way he kin play bumblebee when he wanna an git him a lil color' honey. He's okay. When he wanna be.

I make us sammages, nex he wanna eat his on the livin room rug, an I gotta tell him bout my rug bein too nice fer eatin on.

We done eatin, I tell Jimmy I gotta red-up. He lissen t'the recordplayer an jes layin roun lookin pritty an cute and behavin hisseff okay.

Reddin up give me a chance t'do me some considerin. I git out the lectrick sweeper an all an git t'work, an that give me a chance t'consider how I tol' Madam I is sick, an then that crazy-ass Francine, she pop in an find me wiff my Jimmyboy burgler.

That Francine, she gittin nuttier an nuttier. Maybe cause she gittin so ol. She thirty, gotta wear a bra an all, no tellin what she might do nex.

Course, she ain gonna tell Madam bout me an Jimmy. No. Cause Madam alla time givin her hell bout runnin roun wiff them crazy White girlfrien's. Madam git mad cause Francine come t'work all worn-out an hopped up.

So Francine ain gonna tell Madam nothin. What she gonna do, she gonna blab her big mouff t'the other cats. She got her a big mouff an she gotta talk.

She gonna tell them other cats I got me a White
boyfrien', is how come I ain workin. Yeah, tha's what
Francine gonna do.

She-it! Francine do that, them other cats git all
fuss up counta I meet Jimmy in the cathouse. They
gonna wanna git them some o'my loot, gonna tell me
I is too young t'be on my own.

Nex, Madam gonna hear bout it, an she gonna
wanna move me back in her partmin in the cathouse.
Specially she find out I gotta do that blade fetchin
jes t'git me my weekend hunner. Yeah!

Ooh-wee! Sure got me some plain an fancy considerin t'do.

I'm goin along, cleanin an considerin an makin the
bed, I say t'myseff, I say, Girl maybe you go on in
an work t'night, leave Jimmy here an come on home
t'morra an jes take Sunday off.

But she-it! I can' stan t'think o'all them mothahless
Joe College one-eyes I'm gonna haff t'work on, I go
t'work.

Most o'the time, I don' mind goin t'work. Fack, I
kinda look forwar' t'workin, most o'the time. But
Gee-zuz! Most o'the time, I don' make me no swingin
turnabout weekend hunner, an turnon doin it.

Sides, he is all paid up fer a whole weekend now.
Yeah! I got me some plain an fancy considerin t'do.

I say t'myseff, Jimmy stay here all night an behave
hisseff okay, fine. Sep, he ain gonna wanna do that!
No, he is gonna wanna go. He ain the sittin roun
kind. Specially wiff no tee vee so's he kin watch them
shootin shows.

Considerin an considerin, an cleanin an cleanin, I
gits an idea. I say t'myseff, Girl thing you gotta do is,

you gotta give yer trick somethin t'do, meantime you go on int'work. I say, Now what the hell kin I give him t'do?

An then I say, I kin give him Madam car t'drive! Yeah!

He gonna like that! He kin drive roun some, then he come back an I kin finish givin him his hunner weekend t'morra.

See, Madam, she got this great big ol blackass car, she keep roun my partmin house, an she give me the key cause I can' drive yet an I ain got no permit anyhow. She keep it here cause she don' wanna keep it in Niggertown. An when she wannt git us cats some place fer some outside party, like roun leckshun time, she call up an tell me t'give the key t'Jackie an Jackie drive us.

Jackie done been t'high school, an even some t'college, an she kin drive real good. Yeah, real real good. Sep when she shootup wiff H or git too high on weed, an then Madam fraid Jackie drive that mothahless car int'some pole or somethin.

Course, Jackie, she ain no junkie. She mostly on'y smoke pot, but oncet in awhile she like t'shootup jes fer a lil change. She do her a lotta fatass book readin too, oncet in awhile.

Anyhow, Jackie is already got her a Ford car an she don' wanna drive Madam car nohow. Tha's what she say, but Madam, she don' wanna take no chances, cause last car Madam got, Jackie run him int'some truck. Tha's when Madam give me the key t'keep.

So I got Madam car key. Yeah!

I finish reddin up, I say, Hey Jimmy Honey, you like t'drive?

He say, Huh?

I say, Kee-ryess! I ask you, you like t'drive.

He say, Car?

I say, Yeah man, car.

He say, You mean, Automobeeel?

I say, You think I mean Tee-eee Vee-eee?

He look real funny. He say, You gotta car?

I say, I got Madam car. I tell him bout it.

He say, Wow!

Yeah! He say that! He look real funny, scratch his head, start mumblin crissmiss crissmiss crissmiss.

I say, Baby I gotta go t'work t'night counta Francine seen us.

He wrinkle up his face an jes look dum.

I try t'tell him wha's gonna happen, I don' go t'work t'night, but he so rump-thumpin knuckle-headed dum I can' git thru.

He say, Where's the car?

I say, Hol' yer ass! I say, I give you the key, you promise t'come back here when yer done drivin? You sleep here agen, Lover, an we have some more fun t'morra.

I dam near gotta ack it out t'make him unnerstan.

Then he say, Yeah yeah yeah! An he look real happy.

I say, You promise?

He say, Yeah yeah yeah! He say, Crissmiss crissmiss crissmiss!

I say, Okay. Go easy, man.

He git up an start lookin out the winda. He say, Where's the car.

I say, Right down there. I show him where it's restin.

He say, Crissmiss. He say, Kryessler Peereal!

He git all fuss up now, bout drivin Madam car. He lookin at me an lookin out the winda an lookin at me agen. He laughin.

I'm glad I done my considerin. I say, I likes t'see you happy, Loverboy. I wanna see you a hunner dollah happy. I wanna see you a hunner hunner dollah happy happy!

Nex, he start in buggin me. Seem like he so godam happy, he wanna play him nother movie scene. Phew! I ain in no mood fer that perten crap jes now, so I shilly shally.

I shilly shally off an go back t'cleanin agen, jes t'git away, but he follow me roun.

Ain right, me hangin him up like that, but I do anyhow. Jes because!

Way I git him off my ass is, I send him back t'that mothahless car.

I say, Jimmy you wanna go fer a ride?

He say, Ride?

Yeah! We gotta go all over it agen counta he so Gee-zuz dum.

But I git him t'unnerstan, an he is all set t'go ridin. He say, Yeah yeah yeah, an like that.

She-it! He so muddlefuggin fuss up, I fraid he gonna run out bareass an jump in Madam car right now.

I say, Jimmy first we gotta git dress'.

He say, Yeah, course we do.

We do.

Time we do, it gittin dark out. Good thing. Don' look right, Whiteboy an Pickaninny girl runnin roun the street. Fack, some folks livin this partmin house, they alla time callin the law cause so many Whitefolks goin in an outta here. They don' like Whitefolks nohow.

Some Nigger's dam near's nasty's some Whitefolks they don' like. Sometime I think on'y thing color' bout them is they skins, cause they hearts is spiteful Whitefolks hearts. Piss on them Niggers!

We bout ready t'go out the door, Jimmy git jittery agen. He say maybe we oughtta seprate, meet at the car.

I spect we oughtta. Don' look right, Whiteboy an Pickaninny girl walkin outta some partmin house side by side.

Yeah! Sides, nother thing! Can' let none o'them other cats see us gettin in Madam car t'gether, even they do see me walkin out. But Kee-ryess! They better not see me neither, or my ass'll be mud!

I say, Okay. I say, You go on down an walk t'the corner.

He say, What corner?

Fer oncet he ask a smart queshun. I say, Billboard Corner.

Then he right back an givin me huh huh huh agen. I say, Gee-zuz Jimmy! Don' start that godam queshun crap all over agen, *please*!

An he look hurt. He say, He don' know what corner is the Billboard Corner.

I take him t'the winda an show him.

He jes git done lookin outta that winda. Billboard Corner right there!

I say, Jimmy wonner you still livin, you so dam much dum dum dum!

He give me his wrinkle look agen.

Ooh-wee! I spect I hurt his feelins agen, but Kee-ryees! Good thing he got all that jack an he is White! He Nigger an broke, he most likely spend his whole livelong life in jail, he so dee-diddly-dum-diddly-dum!

He finish being dum, he go on out the door an down an I see him walkin along down the street t'the Bill-board Corner. I watch, see he do okay. No tellin what he might do, he such a muddlehead.

I go on down then, an git in Madam car. Jackie kin drive him real fine, but I can'. He so big, I kin hardly see out. I do jes what Jackie do, an Madam car start okay. I driv him oncet jes a lil ways so I know how he do when I push the peddle. I off the brake an make the lil line go on *D*, and I push the peddle real real soff.

He go! Yeah! He like t'go t'the moon!

But I push the brake peddle an he stop, an I git him goin right agen, an I push the other peddle, an he go, an then I push the brake peddle an he stop.

Ooh-wee Skinny Minnie! Ain easy drivin Madam car, specially when you don' know how! But I make it t'the corner okay, an Jimmy is there. I can' git him hind that wheel fast enuff. He there, he know what t'do.

Nex, he push that peddle so hard, my head like t'come off!

I say, Gee-zuz Jimmy! Take it easy!

But he don'. He go t'drivin Madam car like it ain never been driv! He comin at this here stoplight like he is gonna go on red. That ain right counta them other cars is goin cross-wise, counta they is on green. I bout she-it right now!

But he stop!

Yeah! On'y trouble is, he stop so fuggin fast, I *don'* stop! I slide off the seat an land on the floor!

I'm sittin there, Jimmy laughin, I say t'myseff, Girl maybe best you stay on the floor so's you can' see what the hell you gonna hit.

But I git back up, jes when Jimmy push that *go* peddle agen, so's I fly on back a-gin the seat.

I say, Kee-ryess Jimmy. Where the fug you goin?

He laugh and he say, He don' know *where* he is goin, he's jes a-goin.

I say t'myseff, I say, Yeah man! You makin more sense than you know you is!

I say, Jimmy I gotta go t'Madam an work t'night. We can' go too far.

He say, He git me t'Madam okay. He say, Then he go take him a ride.

I say, Okay. I say, Then you go on back an sleep in my bed.

He say, Sure! Like, way he say it, he say, Sh-ur-ur-ur!

I don' like the way he say it. He so fuss up bout drivin Madam car, I beginnin t'git a lil worried. I beginnin t'think maybe he gonna take off fer the moon in Madam car. But she-it! I spect he drive roun some, he git tired an come on back. Yeah! He drive roun awhile, make him tired o'drivin.

I say, Jimmy I go t'Madam, you go take you a nice long drive. You take you a nice hiway drive. Okay?

He smile nice an laugh, an he start sayin, Yeah yeah yeah!

He be okay. Long's he don' go nowhere he gotta

think, he be okay. He git int'trouble somehow and he start ackin dum agen, then *I* got trouble!

I say t'myseff, Girl come t'think of it, you is takin you one big fatass chance, lettin this dum Whiteboy drive Madam car.

On'y thing is, I'm beginnin t'like this mothah, now I got his jack. Sides, he ain got him his weekend hunner worff yet, so how kin I jes kick him out? I wanna make it so's he gittin his hunner worff o'me, we is boff enjoyin it an gittin along invessment-fine, like Jackie an her invessment do. An if he gonna be my invessment, I gotta treat him good. You jes can' go makin invessment an then kick his ass out. You gotta give some an git some. I give him better time than he spect t'git *now*, he gonna wanna come roun agen soon wiff more loot, which I is gonna git by givin him nother fine time.

Yeah!

Nex, we drivin along okay, fast an jittery but okay anyhow, I say t'myseff, Girl pritty soon be time fer you t'go t'work, an Saterday night you ain gonna git much chance t'eat.

I say, Jimmy buy me somethin t'eat.

He wrinkle up a lil, then he say, Where?

That ain such a dum queshun, considerin we ain the same color.

I say, I know where. Ham House.

He say, Where?

I say, Hell man, ain you never heard o' Ham House? It's in Niggertown, on the radio alla time. I say, You know where is Niggertown?

He say, He think he do.

I say, It's where all the down-n-out Niggerfolks lives.

He say, Where the cathouse is?

I say, Yeah man, tha's Niggertown. Tha's where Ham House is.

He say, Oh. Then he say, Wha, Who, Hee, Ho! He say, No we can' go *there*! He say, What'f somebody see us in Madam car?

Yeah!

I say, Yer right man. Maybe somebody tell Madam we got her car out. How come you git so bright so quick?

He say, I got time, he kin drive us out the hiway an we kin git somethin t'eat out there.

I say, Okay, jes's long's I git t'Madam by ten or leven.

So we go. An I ain jes's a-foolin we go! We go like she-it thru a tin horn. Jimmy swing that black-ass car ont'the hiway, and he push that cottinpickin peddle down, an ooh-wee! We go so fast I begin t'feel like I been smokin cigarets. Yeah! I git dizzy lookin at them lights jes a-whizzin by us, an us jes a-goin like the whole worl' ain here no more, an we is jes a-floatin off t'land some place.

Gee-zuz!

I say, Jimmy you slow down or I'm gonna take this car right back!

But he jes laugh an keep passin everythin in sight. I spect he know I ain gonna take the car back cause he seen I can' hardly drive a-tall. Course, he don' gotta be so bright t'see that, way I drive this car t'the corner.

So I say, Lover please slow down. I say, Police gonna git us, you don' slow down. Police git us, they gonna toss yer ass in jail an throw away the key!

Counta you bein a burgler, I say.

Good thing he still playin perten he's a burgler. No tellin what mightta happen.

He slow down. Bout this time, we done gone by so many eatin joints, we dam near upstate.

She-it! He jes a-sittin there drivin an smilin at his own drivin. He dam near's happy's if he foun him a bran new boom boomin tee vee. Kee-ryess! Jackie never drive like that. How come he can' drive cool like Jackie? Jackie drive us fast on the hiway but she don' take off fer the moon like he do. An she don' sit there wiff no hotass grin on her face neither. Jimmy drive like this car gonna show a tee vee lawman an start goin raie raie, boom boom. Kee-ryess!

I say, Jimmy you make this godam thing stop fore we git alla way upstate. Huh?

He say, He gonna stop nex place.

Nex place! *Which* nex place? Places jes a-whizzin by.

I say, Jimmy stop this dee-diddly-godam car! Stop him right now!

He laugh. Gittin unner my skin, way he laugh.

But he stop. Yeah! I bout crap, but he do.

Then, nex dum thing he do, he git out an walk! Yeah! He git out an take off walkin back along the hiway!

He take a couple-a steps, I out an the hell affer him. I say, Jimmy where the hell you goin?

He say, T'git somethin t'eat. He say, Don' you wanna eat?

I say, Yeah I wanna eat, but——

An he say, He gonna go an bring us back somethin t'eat.

I say, Gee-zuz man! We come alla way out here an you gonna *walk*?

He say, Yeah he gonna walk. He say, We can' boff go in, so he is goin. He knows this real good place lil way back, an he goin there.

I say, But man, you gonna leave me *here*, all alone?

He say, Sure he gonna leave me. He say, He comin right back. He say, He is goin t'this White place, I can' come.

An he takes off.

Me, I is there all all alone! Yeah! He leave my poor Nigger Pickaninny me all alone on that madass hiway in this great big blackass Madam car I can' even drive! I don' know if I gonna she-it or cry! But I git back in that car an lock all the doors an all, and I sit there. I jes on'y do nothin but sit ass right down the hell there, lookin up ahead at this bigass billboard night sign jes a-blink talkin real weird, wiff all them cars a-whizzin by me on the hiway, goin t'the moon. Yeah! Them cars jes a-goin like they is goin t'the moon! Jes like on them tee vee shows I seen when I was a wee tiny Pickaninny, back fore I quit lookin that glassface in the eye, them shows where police is chasin robbers on the hiway, jes a-chasin an chasin. I spect any minit some car gonna pull up an stop an some mean lookin Whiteman gonna git out wiff a gun an shoot my poor ol blackass Pickaninny me right in the face like he is some mean tee vee lawman! I is so flipfloppin scared, I feel like I'm gonna pee down my leg. All them cars goin by like that, an me all all alone, an everybody jes goin like they is mad at everybody else, an all them muddle heads jes fulla that tee vee raie raie boom boom noise, an that up-ahead night sign jes a-blink talkin away, I jes sure somethin tee vee terrible gonna happen fore Jimmy gits back.

An Gee-zuz! He gone so lo-o-o-o-ng! Time he git back, I near outta my black hide.

I say, Jimmy you fay burgler bastid, how come you leave me out here so dam long?

He say, He don'. He say, He on'y gone five minits.

She-it! But I so godam hard-titty scared, I'm glad t'see the dum mothah anyhow. Fack, I so glad t'see him, I move on over real close an cozy up side him. Kee-ryess, my ol teeth jes a-chatterin somethin terrible!

I say, Jimmy don' you never never run off like that an leave my poor ol Pickaninny me the hell out here on no Whiteman hiway.

He laugh! Yeah! He don' laugh like he laugh before. He laugh like some drunk in the cathouse. He laugh, Heah heah heah!

Ooh-wee! I *so* fuggin mad! Bout this time, I so mad I kin scratch his eyes out. On'y thing stop me, I can' drive. I kin drive, that dum heah-heah ain got no eyes.

Good thing I can' drive. Way I is, all I kin do is cry. He go t'give me a hamberger, an all I kin do is sit there lookin that Whiteplace hamberger wiff them madass mothahless muddlehead moon-goin White-folks cars tearin along wiff all them tee vee boom bommin Whitefolks drivin 'em, an that up-ahead blink-talkin, an all I kin do is cry! I cry so hard, I can' hear nothin, an I can' even see that hamberger. I cry so hard, my poor ol Pickaninny heart feel like it gonna choke me.

Jimmy, he ack all worried, he see me cryin like that. I cryin an cryin! Nex, I hear him tryin t'talk sweet talk, fer Kee-ryess sake! Yeah! He try, but he can'. He ain no better at talkin sweet than he was at playin nice. He can' play nice an he can' talk sweet!

Fack, come t'think of it, that dum bastid can' even *pay*! I even gotta fetch me a blade fore he pay!

I cry an cry, thinkin that, an then I say t'myseff, Girl you done it now. You done it fer sure. Here you is wiff some tee vee Whiteboy, can' pay, can' play, can' even talk sweet when he wanna! I say t'myseff, Girl you fug up somethin terrible! You shoulda throwed his dum ass out soon's you got his hunner. You done that, you don' find yerseff like this.

Then I say, She-it! I say, Jimmy quit tryin t'talk like you don' know how t'talk. I say, Yer so cram fulla raie raie boom boom shootin an fightin an killin an big-word noise, you jes can' do nothin else!

He shut up. I don' think he really know what I'm talkin bout, but he shut the hell up, an he eat his hamberger.

My mouff too fulla cry t'eat jes yet. But I stop cryin an git back t'better considerin.

Nex, Jimmy take off drivin agen, but now he is drivin better. He goin wiff everybody else, so it don' seem so weird. It like when Jackie drivin us some-place. On'y thing missin's music. I turn on the radio, but we so way far out, I can' git no Niggertown station, so I turn it back off.

An I git that hamberger in my belly. I don' much feel like it, but I do.

Jimmy, he's lookin sad. He lookin all wrinkle up agen.

I say t'myseff, Girl maybe he do feel bad bout leavin you, you cryin like you done. Maybe he jes can' help hisseff, he can' talk sweet. I say t'myseff, Maybe he ain never had nobody talkin sweet t'him, is how come he can' talk sweet hisseff. Maybe all he know is that glassface son-a-bitch wiff all that perten crap, an all them soljers an rockits an bombs an junk. An that mothahless news which ain nothin but big-word noise, wiff them tee vee men talkin up an down like they is preachin, an them dum lookin Whitechicks singin bout beer like they's all hot up fer beer boy-frien's.

Affer all that, he ack like he wanna talk sweet. She-it! How he ever gonna learn t'talk sweet wiff all that crap jes a-boomin in his ear an lookin him eye-t'eye? Seem like he already drown hisseff in that great big noisey pile o'crap.

Sides, maybe he got him some fay girlfrien', don' know how t'play nice. Maybe he don' even git him no pussy neither, a-tall! Maybe he gotta come t'the cathouse t'git him some pussy, counta havin him such a tee vee terrible girlfrien'.

Could be. Way he ack, could dam well be.

Madam say, A man don' git him no pussy fer a long time, he is gonna ack bad an mean. He is gonna git mad at the whole worl'. He is gonna git so he can' ack no way sep nasty.

Yeah! Madam say that!

Maybe poor ol Jimmy come int'the cathouse las' night, he like that. Maybe tha's his trouble. I gotta teech him how t'go slow an pritty when he wanna play turnabout. Yeah!

But that ain right, cause I ain never been teeched

neither, an I ain never been *that* dum. I jes pick up doin an lissenin t'the other cats talkin, like anybody else.

Kee-ryess! How kin he be's tee vee dum's he is?

Course, he dum, ain his fault, I spose. Maybe he jes born dum. Maybe he jes born Whitefolks dum, so's he kin lissen t'that big-word tee vee preachin, an so's he kin dig that shootin an fightin an ack mean an maybe even kill somebody human, but not so's he kin do nothin much else, like talk sweet an play nice an consider wiffout gittin all muddlefug up.

Yeah! I consider an consider, an I say t'myseff, Girl ain his fault, he jes don' know no better.

This here a funny ol worl' wiff all kinda folks. Some smart, some dum, some White, some Black, some rich, some poor, an plenty in between.

Alla time I is considerin this, an considerin what a sorry ol White worl' I'm livin in, we gittin closer an closer t'Niggertown. Nex, I look up an we dam near t'Madam.

I say, Hey Jimmy, stop an let me out. I kin walk from here.

He say, Okay.

He stop.

Then he say, Kitten . . . An he soun real sad. He say, Kitten I'm sorry bout leavin you. I di'n know it was gonna upset you like that.

I say, Fergit it, Jimmy.

I say t'myseff, Kee-ryess! No wonner you don' know, Whiteboy. So much you don' know, it ain even funny. So godam everlastin much you don' know, it make we wanna start in cryin all over agen!

But he keeps on talkin, like. He say, Kitten . . .

An he look real real sad. He say, I don' know, an he say, like, Wha, Who, Hee, Ho, like that agen, an then he jes peter out an stop talkin an we jes is on'y doin nothin but sittin.

I say, Well man, I gotta go.

He say, Yeah. It dam near leven.

I say, Kee-ryess!

An I quick jump out an run.

I really honestly think that little colored prostitute should be psychoanalyzed at the first opportunity. I mean, of course, ha ha, I realize that's absurd—psychoanalyzing a person like Kitten. What I'm trying to point out is that by this time I was forced (after the next equally fantastic event occurred) to come to a rather drastic conclusion. To wit:

She was deeply disturbed. I mean, deep deep down in her subconscious mind, such as it was, she was, well, she was—I'll say it—she was *psycho*!

I mean it! She, for gosh sakes, was a case for a mental institution! Not only was she practically unpatriotic and entirely immoral—not to mention the language she used—(I mean, I can't possibly repeat in words, either out loud or in print, the utter and complete profanity she poured forth upon certain emotional occasions) (occasions which became increasingly more numerous as our little misadventure progressed)—not only that, but she was also unbalanced. This, too, became increasingly clearer to me as my investigation progressed.

(Progressed? That's not exactly the word for it. It *di*gressed! Yes, that's more accurately what it did.)

But her language—which, as I mentioned, I can't possibly repeat—became almost intolerable. I was shocked back at the house of ill repute when I first heard her speak, but that was nothing compared to what came later! For instance (and I don't wish to dwell on the subject, of course, I only want to present enough for the sake of verisimilitude)—for instance, when she was wrestling with her TV set, trying to throw it out the window, for gosh sakes—an incident I believe I've adequately outlined—she kept shouting (and I herewith paraphrase, of course) such things as : 'Mother fornicator !' and 'Mother fornicate this,' and 'Mother fornicate that,' and also used other unmentionable phrases and words.

Now don't get me wrong. I'm fully aware that she was uneducated and all that, and I'm far from prejudiced, as I'm sure you have certainly surmised by now, Dear Reader. (How could I possibly find myself in such a predicament if I were the least bit prejudiced?) But that language she used, that constant barrage of obscenities, was too much. Almost. I mean, she wasn't what you could call underprivileged, living in that swank apartment. And swiping my $100 to boot! With her annual income, even after federal taxes (if she paid them), she must certainly know that civilized people just don't constantly keep uttering profanities. On certain occasions, I couldn't even separate the conversation from the profanity. She just jabbered both out at once, kind of ran them together. Intertwined them, so to speak.

But, back to the most fantastic incident of all—the tactical mistake she made, giving me my capital and grand opportunity.

Unbelievable as it may seem, she had a Chrysler Imperial! I mean, she didn't *own* it, apparently. In fact, she couldn't even drive it. It belonged to some underworld character—that much I was able to deduce—whom she referred to as the Madman, or some such nickname.

Well, it was shortly after she'd made sandwiches (fantastic, of course—about three inches thick, with vast assortments of lunchmeats, lettuce, tomatoes, onions, pickles, mustard, hard-boiled eggs, the works). We'd eaten, and she hadn't insulted my masculinity this time by insisting I do the dishes. (As a matter of strict fact, there weren't any dishes to do.) She sort of deserted me for a time, just took out a vacuum cleaner and went to work housecleaning. And this to music! I mean, we had the hi fi going, playing those absurd records of hers, and she went through the motions of housecleaning to the rhythm of whatever happened to be playing. Silly, I realize, but that's what she did.

Meanwhile, I sat and pondered my problem : How to reclaim my stolen $100.

Then, like a highly intellectual poetic inspiration from the devine blue, it came. She wanted—repeat wanted—yours truly to drive this gangster's Imperial, just take it out for a spin, I suppose, and blow the gunk out of its huge engine.

Well, this idea appealed to me immediately, and on several levels of consciousness. First, my uncle Ben has an Imperial— (Ben's a higher-up in business but has always been jealous of Dad, because Dad's a professional person with high ideals and all, and so makes so much more money than Ben, so Ben tries to put on the dog, so to speak, by buying showy things; ergo his Imperial)—which I love to drive. I mean, our Caddy (which we use only to drive to the theatre and restaurants and church, places like that) handles well. Very well. But that Imperial —wow! You're maybe out on the turnpike, just cruising along about 85 miles an hour, and here comes some joker in a Jag or something foreign like that— just wheels up along side of you and is about to shame you. Ha! You just goose that old Imp's accelerator and . . . No more Jag! Yes sir, it's bye-byes. You can dust just about anything moving with that Imperial. I mean it!

That's point number one.

Point number two is where the poetic inspiration comes in. No sooner had she mentioned her desire (that I take the Madman's car, as she called it, out for a spin) than I was thunderstruck by this brilliant idea.

Namely, that now I had her! Yes, but absolutely! Once I got in the cockpit of that beautiful machine, the shoe would be on the other foot, so to speak.

Again I wish I were a paid professional writer, this time so I could describe to you in instantaneous and beautific, the sheer thrilling wonder of it when my brain connected with that idea. I mean, no sooner had she mentioned that she wanted me to drive that car than I was, like, *inspired*!

A moment before I had been wondering, trying to put myself in her place so I could imagine where she might hide that $100 she had stolen, and now everything fell into place, but beautifully.

Well, beauty marred by but one problem: It was quite clear by now that this professional prostitute of another color had fallen in love with yours truly. And had done this, no doubt, on the assumption that I was a burgler, a fellow member of the underworld community.

Well, I had been afraid that would happen. I mean, I'm not the sort to go tampering with any girl's basic emotions, even if she is a lady of ill repute and of another color. I like to be decent about such matters at all times. But, on the other hand, this was a special case, sort of. After all, $100 hung in the balance, suspended, and now that I had my capital, the matter boiled down to one thing: Supply and demand!

Besides, even if she was in love with me, she was what she was, and the sort she was fall in and out of love at the drop of a hat. (As a matter of hard cold fact, it had also become clear to me by this time that she had an unhealthy and crude concept of the sacred procreative act. I mean, it was like she had never seen one single solitary documentary movie on the subject. She was simply full of the sort of attitudes toward the subject our better periodic organs, like LOOK, constantly label *sex fictions,* for gosh sakes!)

I mean, she was incapable of profound feelings. She was quite obviously a shallow woman who lived a tremendously fast life, and being a professional lady, what harm could I do her?

All's fair in love and war, as they say. So now, it was off to the races; the die had been cast, you might say.

Anyway, we went riding. I wasn't certain what my next step would be. I mean, I had my longrange tactical plan of procedure and kept it flexible so I could alter my course quickly. I knew one thing for sure: her motive. And that, after all, is important. Her motive, quite simply, was that she wanted me to come back and sleep in her apartment, wanted me to be there when she came home in the morning.

You see, (I've completely neglected to disclose an important turn of events—a change of plans) she had called the syndicate earlier, as I mentioned, and reported off duty. Then, in the middle of everything, she switched, and announced she intended to work that night. (Work being, possibly, an inaccurate word for it, ha ha.)

Anyway, riding : Right off the bat she said she was hungry. How she could possibly be hungry after that huge sandwich on top of that gigantic breakfast at noon was beyond me. I mean, she was just a little person, no more than five feet two or three inches tall. But I could force a hamberger, if need be, so I had no objections.

Hence, we went in search of food. Which isn't such a simple matter when you're with a woman of another color. I mean, they have their places and we have ours.

Though, don't get me wrong here : I'm all for the Supreme Court decision and integration of the schools and all; I'm not a Segregationist by any means. But, like I said, they have their places and we have ours. To eat at, I mean.

But she suggested we go back to the rundown neighborhood in which was located the ill repute house. She mentioned some dive named the Ham House.

Obviously that was out. Good grief ! I could just see myself walking into an all-colored place in the middle of that Negro substandard district with her, and with all those evil-looking Negroes just standing there doing nothing, staring at us. The very thought of it gave me the chills. Why, we'd be lucky to escape with our lives!

So, at my suggestion, we drove out Route 707.

Of course, all this came after she almost wrecked the Imperial. I mean, since we certainly couldn't be seen together, I went out and waited on the corner and she followed, got in the car and drove it to the corner.

But I shouldn't say *drove*. I broke into a cold sweat when I saw it: That great, shining, beautiful Imperial with her at the wheel. Right off the bat she darn near rammed it into the side of her apartment building, then she cut back and came about an inch from sideswiping parked cars along the other side of the street—all the time just creeping, but in fits and jerks, zigzagging back and forth, and all in all making a complete and utter mockery of the safe-driver laws.

But, miraculously, she did reach the corner without crashing into something and I climbed into the old cockpit and we were okay.

That is, the car and I were. She wasn't really at ease in an automobile, being barely civilized, and slid right off the seat at the first stoplight we came to.

And, just like a woman, she nagged. I, however, didn't let her nagging bother me; just revved up all eight and cruised. I wanted to see how she would handle and when we hit the highway, I did. She passed everything on the road, clipping along at 70 with ease and still with plenty of pedal left. (Highway 707 is usually a bit crowded during the day and evening, so I waited until later when I had more road to myself to really test drive her.)

Besides, Kitten's deep subconscious disturbance came to the surface during that drive, and I couldn't help being concerned. After all, I didn't want to end up in some gangster's car with a complete psychotic of another color on my hands.

So we stopped up the road a bit from the MW Drivein and I got out to walk back and buy us a couple of burgers.

Then—Bamb!

That's when I became completely convinced that she had a deep mental disturbance.

Right off the bat she wanted to come with me. To the Drivein, I mean. She wanted to just get out and walk back along the highway with me, walk right in and we'd be there together, and order up, just like nothing!

I finally convinced her that this would be impossible and left her in the car, thinking she was back to normal.

But . . .

I was only gone a few minutes. When I returned, she was sitting there in the far corner, cowering like a wild animal. She was scared silly! I got in and the next thing I knew, she was crawling all over me. She just shot across the seat and wrapped her arms around me and sat there shivering, giving off with more of her profanity and unbelieveable mutilations of the English language.

I thought : Gracious, JC, how did you ever manage this? How did you ever manage to get yourself in this gangster's classy car, out here on Route 707, with this paid professional colored girl of ill repute having a nervous breakdown?

Well, all I can say is, it's a good thing I kept my longrange tactical plan of procedure flexible. I mean, I was quick to comprehend that she didn't suspect I was still in business, just took it for granted that now that she had my money, I would submit to do her bidding, and not even entertain thoughts of getting my money back.

And *that* gave me direction!

But first, I had to calm her down, for gosh sakes! I had to snap her out of it before it reached any advanced stage of psychosis. So I did. I talked her out of her maladjustment and by the time we arrived in the slum district, in which her ill repute house was located, she was normal. Well, *almost* normal. She had simmered down to a pout. Which was an improvement over the uncooperative attitude she displayed at first.

So I let her out not far from the ill repute house and she walked the remaining distance. I felt sorry for her, in a way. Even if she was a thief, I felt sorry for her because she was obviously so psychologically disturbed. I left her wondering how a person could get along in life, being that deeply disturbed. I was even tempted to send to the National Advertising Council for that pamphlet about dealing with one's emotions in the modern world, in the hope that such enlightenment would benefit her.

But that was out. Besides being psycho, she was unintelligent and illiterate, practically, and probably wouldn't understand it anyhow. Which was unfortunate, of course.

But I had more important concerns. I still had the key to her apartment in my pocket, and the tough-mindedness to know that my money was one of two places : On her person or in her apartment.

I had a hunch it was the latter.

However, before going back to her place, I test drove that mighty Imperial. By this time, it was past 11 o'clock at night, so Route 707 was relatively clear of local traffic. I buzzed out there in about half an hour and away I went.

Man! Did that baby *move*! I mean! I came out of this merge at about 60—a graceful 60—then floored it, and—wham!

Is there any sensation in the world which surpasses the one when you have a great and powerful car— where you and it become married in one glorious blaze of blinding speed? Christmas! If there is, I'd like to know about it. I mean, what a piece of machinery that beautiful Imperial was! I could hardly believe my eyes. That speedometer needle just sort of leaned over all the way and landed on 120, and still it felt like she had more in reserve.

And, to this day I believe I got more out of her. But how much more I'll never know for sure, because the needle stuck. It just landed on 120 and, for gosh sakes, *stayed*!

Even when I slowed down. Which I did a few minutes later, because even though we have a state senator living next door to us (at home), I certainly didn't want to get stopped by the police and involved in politics and have my present circumstances publicized to the family. I mean, I'd have one heck of a time explaining to Dad what I was doing out on Route 707 in some gangster's Imperial, for crying out loud!

So, after my little spin down the highway, I drove back and went to her apartment to give it a thorough and scientific search. I thought : After all, JC, you can save that poor little colored psychotic further psychological disturbance if your hunch is correct and you are able to unearth your money in her place and do this without invoking the law of supply and demand per your ultimate tactical plan.

Time I git t'Madam, I'm feelin so blue, I jes ache. I say t'myseff, Girl you gotta fergit all bout that fer now, but I can' hardly make myseff fergit cause I so cram fulla spiteful Whitefolks crap an I got me so many worries, I *is* sick. I so achin, I feel like my whole inside-an-out-Pickaninny me jes one great big sore.

First, I gotta go tell Madam I *ain* sick. I tell her I got better affer I call her. Alla time I'm tellin her this, I feel sicker an sicker.

Then I go on back t'the dressin room, other cats all there. An nex, I git t'wonnerin, did them cats see Madam car was gone when they took off fer work? Ooh-wee! I wonner that, I git so scared my belly hurt.

Jackie, she come on over t'me an don' say nothin, jes look. Jackie an Madam on'y folks I got leff. They boff alla time lookin out fer my blackass. Madam, she real bright, alla time readin them fatass books. Jackie, she bright too. She mostly either readin or weedin, don' shootup much. She readin, I kin tell counta she look haff mean an haff funny. She weedin, she look happy an gone. She shootup, she look plain gone. I kin see she been readin.

She say, So yer makin yer first invessment, eh.

I say, How the hell you know?

She say, She was gonna come on in my partmin t'day but she hear some Whiteman inside, so she go away. She say, Sides, Francine been blabbin bout my trick. Francine been sayin he look like he is loaded.

I say, Yeah he loaded, but he nutty too. I tell her I can' unnerstan him an he can' unnerstan me, an he dam near walk out wiffout payin up. I say, But I finally git me my one hunner fer the weekend.

She say, Shhh! She say, Hush up, don' let them other cats hear that. She say, I do right t'git my hunner but now I gotta hush up.

She say, How come I'm here in the cathouse t'night, I got me a weekend t'tend to?

I say, It too fuggin mix up, how come. I can' tell her all at oncet how come. I say, He gonna be my place t'morra, and we gonna finish the weekend t'morra. I say, Mainly I is here counta I'm scared o'them other cats.

An I jes bout ready t'tell Jackie bout Jimmy bein in Madam car, but I say t'myseff, Later I kin tell her that. It too muddlefuggin way up t'talk bout right now.

Nex, that godam Francine start in on me. Yeah! She holler out, Hey Kitten, how you doin wiff yer Whiteboy loverman?

That Francine, she gotta big mouff!

Jackie say, Francine you shut up! You jes mind yer own dam bizness, leave everybody else alone.

Jackie an Francine start in bitchin.

Nex, Madam come in an everybody hush up. Madam say, We got tricks.

We all go on out t'the sittin room, an Kee-ryess! We got this whole army o'fay College Joes, is what we got. So many, ain no room fer sittin. Everybody goin upstairs at oncet.

Upstairs, I talk real nice t'my fay trick, same time I so bellyachin sick an cram fulla spiteful Whiteman tee vee noise an jittery from fightin all day long wiff Jimmy, I bout ready t'bite him steada tend t'bizness. He been drinkin an he look real sad an all wrinkle up. Firs' thing I know, he look at me like I is outta some book he can' unnerstan, an he is sayin, You pritty girl. Wha's yer name?

He say that like he can' believe what he sayin.

I say, Man you look agen. I say, Man I ain pritty. I'm *black*!

I say that, he jes look real dum. Real real dum.

Fer awhile, we git us nothin but College Joes an every last one o'them mothahs recall t'me that tee vee boom boomin an big-word noise. On'y thing I kin do t'ease my achin is start callin they cocks rockits. I tell 'em, Come on Baby, le's launch that rockit!

They laugh at that, dum she-its.

I say t'myseff, I say, One-a these days all you dum moon-goin bastids gonna wake up an find you got nothin but rockitcocks. Yeah! an all yer Whitechicks gonna have steel pussy too, an you ain gonna have no more chillin. Yeah! Us Pickaninnies, don' give one fast crap fer all yer godam moon-goin rockit rackit, we's gonna be the on'y ones leff. Ain gonna be nothin but color' chillin an blackass Pickaninnies, an like that. Yeah! I say that t'myseff.

Time we git that mothahless fay army the hell outta that cathouse, I'm feelin so down an out sorry fer

myseff I can' hardly keep from cryin. We git a time
when no bizness comin in, so I go on in the dressin
room an jes sit a spell. Sit an feel bad.

Seem like everybody else have a good time that
Saterday night. Even Francine havin fun, cause some
Whiteboy slip her a pint fer a tip an she is alla time
sippin on the sly, so she don' give a toot fer nothin. An
Madam, she don' care neither, cause she is feelin
good, counta Detecktiv come in.

Yeah!

See, Detecktiv, he was workin fer the vice squad,
long time ago. Tha's how come him an Madam such
good frien's. Course, Detecktiv ain no detecktiv fer
the law no more. Jackie, she say he is *real* detecktiv
now. He ain workin fer the law counta he git his ass
fire' by the mayor. Yeah! He broke an down an out
an all now, an Madam on'y one keepin him goin.

Sometime, him an Madam go on upstairs an he stay
all night, an boff o'them git t'readin them fatass books.
Out loud, sometime. One time, other cats say, he
come an stay all winter.

This time, Detecktiv come in, him an Madam
git t'talkin an talkin, an cuttin up an all. They's
talkin, couple-a other cats dancin t'the recordplayer,
Francine slippin her sippin, everybody havin fun sep
me.

I'm jes on'y sittin off in the dressin room by myseff,
wonnerin is I ever gonna feel like me agen, an Kee-
ryess!

Nex, I hear this big noise, an I say t'myseff, Gee-
zuz! Here come nother godam fay army. I bout ready
t'run out the back door an jump off the Niggertown
bridge. Yeah! I so blue an all mix up from bein wiff

that dum gee-the-fuggin-Jimmy-burgler all day long, then comin t'work an findin nothin but them everlastin tee vee College Joes, I bout done.

Then I hear this big ol loud yell somebody give, soun like Hay-ae-ae-ae Kitten! Where's my pritty pritty pritty Kitty!

Harry! Yeah! Hairy Harry!

Him an this whole buncha railroad tricks.

Nex, that ol cathouse come alive! Good thing, else I don' know how I ever make it thru that Saterday night.

I gotta tell bout Harry. He jes bout my most favorite trick. Fack, I spect he is!

He work fer the railroad, live in some other town. Him an them other railroadmen come here oncet every so offen, an oncet they inside that door, oohwee!

Firs' time they come, I on'y been workin a week. Fore that, Madam say I is too young. This one, his name Harry, he jes funny's he kin be. He got more mothahhumpin hair on him than I ever did see. He give me the spooks at first, I see all that godam hair all over him, but he like me an wanna go upstairs wiff me an I find he treat me okay. Any time he come affer that, he go up wiff me.

Las' time him an them other railroadmen come, Harry drunk's hell. He carry on wiff Madam, say he wanna line all us cats up a-gin the wall an work his way right down the line. Way he say it make everybody laugh. He don' on'y say it, he ack it out too. Yeah! We all laughin, he tell Madam—like, he ackin like he ain never *seen* me—he say, How much fer Smilin Susie?

An Madam say, She ain fer sale.

An Harry perten like he considerin fer a secon', then he up an run over an grab my ass an scoot upstairs carryin me an yellin he gonna kidnap me. Everybody laugh, way he do it. That time, he pay thirty bum-bums an stay the rest o'the night wiff me.

We talkin that night, I find out he been t'college too but he don' want no Joe College Whitefolks job, so he jes workin fer the railroad. He kin talk real nice an play nice too. He talk big word sometime, but he don' talk no tee vee big-word noise. I talk t'him, he unnerstan what I is sayin.

I tell him bout when I is jes a lil ol Pickaninny orfan an some goofy Whiteman spit on me an go t'kick my ass over the roof. Yeah! Some ol Whiteman do that! No reason, sep my color. An he'd-a kill' me right now, sep affer he spit, I run—*zoom*! He kick an miss an fall down. An then he git up an start chasin my poor ol blackass Pickaninny me down that street an he bout t'catch me an kill me, then some other Whiteman come along an hit him, an I jes on'y keep on runnin fer my poor ol mothahless life.

I tell Harry that, he git tears in his eyes. Yeah! He jes a-layin there, tears slidin down his cheeks int'his ears.

I tell him, Kee-ryess Harry! Ain no use *you* cryin.

But I never knowed no other Whiteman, sep Harry, kin unnerstan what bein Black is. I spect Harry White *out*side, he got him a nice soff warm color' heart inside. I spect tha's how come he kin unnerstan.

Affer I tell him bout myseff when I jes a wee lil thing, his ol hair don' bother me no more, an I start callin him Hairy Harry. An nex time he screw me, I turn on. I turn on wiff Harry most alla time now, we such good frien's.

This Saterday night, I hear him yellin fer pritty Kitty, I come a-runnin outta that dressin room. I ain never been so glad t'see no Whiteman in all my born blackass days.

On'y trouble, bout the time I fly outta that dressin room, in come this new fay army!

Gee-zuz! Kee-ryess! I near cryin all over agen! This the saddes' lookin buncha tee vee fays I ever seen! They so godam sad lookin I know fer sure they got themseffs rockitcocks or cowboy guncocks or knifecocks, or somethin! I jes know!

Madam hush up them railroads so's they don' chase off them sad-ass College Joes.

Me, I sit ass down in that big chair an jes look mean's I kin look. Most o'them College Joes wanna go up wiff Jackie or Carmie or Ellie, an sometime wiff Francine, but I is fraid one o'them gonna pick me t'night. An I'm feelin so fuggin Whitefolks spiteful, I'm worried some tee vee terrible pick me. I'm gonna lose my Pickaninny sense an scratch his eyes outta his tee vee head steada behavin right.

Bout now, Hairy Harry, an them other railroads, they is jes on'y sittin roun an them College Joes linin up fer Jackie an them other hiyellas. Then Harry he stan up an he say—real loud—he say, Piss on them hiyellas! I want me some lil ol gal straight outta the Africa Jungle! Hey Madam, you got you some Africa Jungle gal?

Yeah! He say that! Real funny, way he say it.

Madam, she look like she gonna she-it!

I up an I say, jes's loud's I kin, I say, Man you

wants *me*! I'm so way out Africa Jungle it ain funny!

Madam, she look like she gonna crap all over agen. Them railroads git t'laughin agen an cuttin up, an them College Joes starts lookin roun sad, but I ain there t'see how sad they ends up lookin, cause me an Harry, we gone upstairs!

Good thing he come that Saterday night, cause by the time he git here, I is so sick a-talkin worry an spite t'myseff bout that crabass White worl', I is feelin so blackass an sorry fer myseff, I dee-diddly-dam well *know* I is from the Africa Jungle. The White-folks Africa Jungle!

Yeah!

Harry, he stay all night. I tell him bout my invessment an how it ain easy makin invessment, an he tell me t'watch my ass, messin roun wiff invessment.

He say, Don' soun right, Jimmy tryin t'walk out wiffout payin up. He tell me t'git Jackie t'help me do my considerin. He say, Later on, when I is fifteen, I kin do all my own considerin. Right now I oughtta git Jackie t'help.

Then I tell him bout Jimmy bein in Madam car. An Harry, he blow up! He go, Wha, Who, Ho, an he say, Yike! He keep sayin like that, an then he tell me I better not tell *no*body bout Jimmy bein in Madam car, not even Jackie.

He say, What kinda car?

I say, Kryessler Peereal.

An he say, *Yike*! He haff laugh an he wrinkle up an he look like he considerin real hard. He say, Criss! He call Jimmy all kinda names an he go on talkin t'hisseff.

I say, Harry I don' mean t'git you all fuss up too.

I say, Kee-ryess! Ain it bad enuff I is in a mess-up wiffout you gittin mess up too?

He laugh. He huff an puff an say he sure hope everythin turn out okay. He say he help me if he could, but he sposed t'leave town in the mornin an there ain nothin he kin think t'do anyhow. He say, Maybe everythin turn out okay.

He git real worried. He ack so worried, I know I done somethin awful dum, givin Jimmy Madam car t'drive.

Nex, Harry say ain nothin t'do now, so we might jes's well git a lil sleep an hope fer the best, so we do. I'm so draggin ass bone tired bout that time, I like t'sleep so deep I die.

Jackie wake me in the mornin.

She laughin when I wake up. She laughin an sayin, Hey Sweetie, you got yerseff a lil green tail!

An I find Harry done laid a ten spot right down tween the cheeks o'my but.

My back was to the wall. My hand had been forced. It was time for a showdown!

Let me begin at the beginning.

Like it says in the Bible, or some place like that: Fight Fire With Fire! I mean, *that*, for gosh sakes, is axiomatic. It's business. Good grief, it's not only business, it's salesmanship on both local and international levels, and foreign policy too.

(To draw an apt analogy, where would this great nation of ours be if everyone were as complacent as some of the jerks I have for frat brothers? I mean, if we didn't deal out tit for tat to those dirty Russians? Answer: We'd be living under the dirty heel of communistic dictatorship! Well, I was in a similar position. Either I give up and let her take my money and keep it, or I show my colors.) (I mean, even though I feared the consequences—to the thin thread from which hung her last ounce of sanity—I had reached a point where I was forced to invoke the law of supply and demand.

I thought: JC, my friend, you no longer have a choice. You must offer to supply her with her gangster's Imperial, thus fulfilling *her* demand, and in return, demand she supply you with the money she's stolen from you, thus fulfilling *your* demand.

Yes, it was that simple.

(Oh I'm quite aware that some jerks and parlor pinks would call this blackmail. But I'm also confident that any intelligent tax-paying, church-going non-communist can appreciate my situation, and readily agree that I was more than justified in thinking of it (the Madman's car) (an apt appelation, ha ha) as a last recourse to retaliatory capability, humanely applied as persuasion rather than force per se.

(I might add, to carry the above stated analogy one step further : Where would the US be without SAC, for instance? Obviously we would disintegrate into a patsey of the communist party which any world power could push around at will.) (I mean, like the Roman Empire, we would decline and fall. We would lose our starch, so to speak.) (Well, look at the English, for crying out loud!) (Not only that, but think of all those brilliant scientists out of work, standing in line for unemployment benefits.)

However, once again like a clever cigarette advertisement, I digress.

Back to the matter of moment : It wasn't there.

I looked high and low. I searched every drawer and every possible hiding place in every closet she had. I emptied out the bathroom cabinet and rummaged through her kitchen cupboards. I pulled clothes from drawers and shook them. I took the bed-clothes off her bed and her mattress out of its mattress cover. I unscrewed the exhaust fan in her kitchen and probed its outer shaft, and did the same to another in the bathroom.

Nothing.

I took into consideration the dim possibility that she might possess a more subtle mind than her illiteracy indicated, and tried to imagine where *I* might hide money I had stolen from a fellow underworld character. Were I in her shoes, I mean. Forthwith, I took every cup and every saucer and every plate out of her cupboards again, but this time looked *between* each and every one. (And she had enough of them, too.) I lifted the top off the watercloset, or whatever it's called, in her bathroom, and I took the glass globe off every overhead light. I fingered every inch of all her window curtains and felt down the cracks beneath the cushions of her couch.

Nothing.

Then I put everything back in its place, so she wouldn't know I'd been there. I wanted to keep the element of surprise on my side. And then—still undaunted—I drove back to the frat house, got the pipewrench from the basement, drove back and got to work on the traps under both the sinks, and also the bathtub. (Which may sound like a simple task to the rank amateur, but it was well past 5 a.m. before I had the pipes back together and her floors back down and the whole general mess mopped up.)

Still nothing.

So, I had reached that point. There was no going back. My back was to the wall, my bridges burned. It was time for a showdown, for the invoking of the law of supply and demand, for the exercise of the planned and well programmed hard sell.

Ah yes, it was well that I had kept my tactical plan of overall procedure flexible. By this, I was at

least able to exhaust all avenues before resorting to
a method which, however realistic and logical to the
legitimate community, might not be fully apprecia-
ted by her. Nor understood, even. I mean, I was afraid
she might *misconstrue*, lacking as she did a formal
education.

However, this was no time to become mushy-minded
about her reaction, whatever it might turn out to be.
It was *onward*—forward, upward, ever onward for
yours truly, JC, in his quest for those one hundred
stolen dollars.

Me an Jackie drivin home in her Ford car, she askin me alla bout Jimmy.

I tell her bout him tryin t'walk out wiffout payin up an how I gotta run, git me a blade fore he pay up.

I don' tell her bout tryin t'keep him from gittin t'the bedroom fer his clothes, counta I'd-a had t'tell her bout me when I thunk how spiteful some Whitemen kin be t'some color girl on'y tryin t'keep her ass bove groun. I thunk that, I got t'cryin an moanin, like, an I even fell down. Alla time I was wonnerin maybe he jes don' know no better. Maybe he so dum he jes don' know, but she-it! Nex thing, he up an run over me an start in gittin dress t'leave. So I had-a fetch me a blade an scoot roun an grab his pants an pay myseff.

I don't tell Jackie I had-a git me a blade.

She say, Kitten where the hell you meet this White-boy?

I say, In the cathouse. An I tell her bout that. I tell her he tryin t'tell me he's a Whiteass burgler an police lookin fer him. I tell her I don' go that crap, but I

164

guess he jes tryin t'set up a weekend, counta he tell me he need some place t'hide.

I know better'n t'tell Jackie I give that dum White-boy my key. I tell her that, she gonna pee her pants. Fer real!

I say, Jackie he seem like he ain so bad sometime I say, He *wanna* be nice. He jes don' know *how*, is all.

She say, That remain t'be seen!

I say, Jackie he dum. Ooh-wee! He so fuggin dum!

She look at me an she say—like this—she say, HE dum! Criss! She say, Kitten ain Madam never tol' you, jack first, fug secen'?

I say, Yeah Madam say that, an I oughtta knowed better, but this here was invessment. I say, I was gonna give an git, steada git an *then* give.

Jackie say, Kitten you gotta learn never truss no-body. Specially them College Joes, an extra specially them what ack like that mothah.

I consider what Jackie say, an I consider Jimmy drivin Madam car, an Kee-ryess! I is fraid t'go on considerin.

I say, Jackie don' seem right, this never truss no-body. I say, Gee-zuz, *I* truss *you*.

She say, You gotta know *who* you kin truss *how much*.

I say, But Jackie you the one tell me bout invess-ment bein *give* an git, *give* an git.

She say, She shoulda tol' me I gotta *know* I is gonna *git* fore I start givin.

Then she start in talkin bout Madam, sayin Madam put me t'work too dam soon. She say, Madam oughtta teech you somethin first.

I say, Madam *try* teechin me readin.

Yeah! Madam do that! I jes a wee tiny lil ol Pickaninny, I is livin wiff me a big black nice ol color' man
and he is treatin me fine. Then he git hisseff 'rested
an go t'jail an I is leff all alone. Then Madam find
me. Yeah! She find me wannerin roun near the police
house cryin fer my man they took away. Madam
come walkin outta police house an see me an pick my
ass up an take me home t'the cathouse. Madam name
me Kitten an I live wiff her till I move on in my
partmin.

Meantime, Madam say she gonna teech me readin
an writtin and like that, an I git all fuss up an hot
t'git at it. She tell me, I kin read, I kin find out bout
all kinda things, like Africa an Whitefolks an Abra-
ham Liggin. But I gits so muddle headed up high
an hot t'do readin, I start in when she ain lookin an
git me so godam mess' up I git cross cause I can'
make out wha's in them fatass books. Nex, she catch
me doin this, she gits me a wee tiny lil ol book an I
git teeched a lil readin in it. But that godam lil book,
oncet I git so's I kin read it, it don' say nothin a-tall,
sep Jack done this an Jill done that, an Gee-zuz! I
jes don' give one fast fart fer what they done, they do
such dum stuff!

Nex, I go on back t'tryin t'read Madam big fatass
books, an I is askin her wha's this word an wha's that
word, an she is tellin me, like, one word, it mean
nother word. Yeah! One word mean nother. Ooh-
wee!

An then I come t'this one big word, mean fug.
Yeah! I come t'this word an I kin tell it gonna mean
somethin *like* fug, but I figure it gotta mean not jes
the *same*.

But Madam, she say, Tha's what it mean. She say, This word, you say Cop You Late, an it mean fug.

I ain never gonna fergit that mothahless word long's my blackass alive! Cop You Late! Kee-ryess! I git me so godam fuss up bout that daddio, I bout flip.

I say, Madam don' it mean somethin else sides jes plain fug?

She say, No.

I say, Madam it mean fug, how come it don' jes *say* fug?

She say, Fug is bad word.

Yeah! She say that! Kee-ryess! Alla time roun that mothahless cathouse everybody sayin fug fug fug, an then Madam go an tell me this fug word is bad. Ooh-wee!

I say, Madam how come it bad?

She say, It like White an Black. She say, like, Cop You Late is like White, an fug is like Black. She say, Cop You Late is like it got loot, an fug is down an out broke.

I say, Madam how come it git t'be down an out broke?

She say, It don' git t'be, it already *be*!

I go on askin *how comes,* then Madam git all fuss up an start in cussin my poor lil ol Pickaninny me. She say, I ain got no mind fer readin. She say, I is *dum* fer readin. She say, Don' mean I'm *plain* dum, jes dum fer readin.

Recall t'me now that mothahless Jimmy. He dum fer considerin, I'm dum fer readin. He kin read them bigass books, I spose, but he jes can' do him no good considerin.

Madam alla time tell me I got me a pritty good

head fer considerin, but I ain never gonna git me no ejukashun counta I is alla time askin such dum quesshuns. Madam quit teechin.

I go on askin her dum queshuns so's when Dolly move on up, Madam so worn out lissenin t'me, she move me the hell outta that cathouse an int'the partmin. Yeah!

Good head fer considerin! Gee-zuz!

Madam find out I leff Jimmyboy drive her big blackass Kryessler Peereal las' night, I ain gonna have no head a-tall!

Jackie drivin, she talkin bout never truss nobody, she say, He gonna be in yer partmin?

I say, Yeah.

She say, What you do wiff yer hunner?

I say, Stick it unner the divan.

An she say, Criss! She say, That daddio in yer partmin an that hunner unner yer divan.

I say, Yeah.

An I feel sick.

Jackie shake her head an smile. She say, Oh well, can' win 'em all.

Then she look at me agen an say, Kitten that hunner there when you git home, you gonna be one lucky lil ol blackass.

I say, Yeah.

An I feel sicker.

I don' tell her nothin bout Francine bustin in. Everythin so way far up already, how m'I ever gonna tell her bout Francine?

She say, Kitten you gotta *learn*! She say, Criss! An she jes shakin her head an drivin along, an I gits t'feelin so jittery sick I can' hardly sit still.

We git home, she ask I want her t'come on in my partmin?

I say, No. I say, First I take a look. Anythin go wrong, I phone fer you.

So we say so long, an I go on in my partmin.

Firs' thing I find, that Jimmy ain there. No!

I bout t'sit right down in the middle o'the livin room an cry my poor ol all-cried-out seff dry. I say t'myseff, Girl you sure got yer dum blackass hung up on the KKK cross now!

Then I recall that hunner an I scoot over an, yeah! It still there unner my divan.

Phew!

I say t'myseff, Girl this hunner been safe here all night, might jes's well leave him be. I can' think-a no place no saffer right now.

Nex, I look out the winda, an ooh-wee Skinny Minnie! Gee-zuz! My wors' nightmare's comin true! Madam car ain there! No! No-oh-oh!

I say, Course maybe he park him some place else.

But hell, I don' hol' much hope. On'y one thing t'do. I gotta take off an hunt roun fer Madam car. I bout t'take off right outta that winda steada ridin the elevator.

I back int'my shoes an coat an got my black hand on that doornob, an—

Dingaling! Phone ring.

I scoot int'the bedroom an I grab that ringin mothah an I say—like my ass's on fire—I say HELLO!

It's him. It that cottinpickin mothahjumpin fight fay burgler bastid. He say, This . . . is . . . Jim.

I say, This is she-it! Where the hell you at?

He say, Never mind where he's at. He say, he got the Kryessler Peereal an he gonna turn it over t'me when he git his one hunner back.

I say, Whaaa?

That fart face done flipflop his Whiteass lid fer sure! Gee-zuz! He gonna play police now. He ain happy jes playin burgler, now he gonna start playin police!

I say, Lover! I say this nice's I kin.

I say t'myseff, Girl you gotta go slow an easy an find out jes what this crazy-ass moon-goin Whiteboy is up to.

I say, Lover where you at now? On'y I say this sweet an soff this time.

An he say, Frae House.

Frae House! I don' know what kinda place is this, but I say—like I know which end is up—I say, Yeah where's that, Baby?

He say, Never mind where's that.

I say, Lover how come you at this here Frae House, how come you ain here wiff me in my place?

He say, He tol' me how come. He got Kryessler Peereal, I got his one hunner. He say, He took Kryessler Peereal counta I took his hunner.

Took! Yeah! He say that! He say, Took *his* one hunner.

I bout squat. But I hang on. I say, Baby how come you wanna be so mean t'one poor lil ol color' girl treat you so good?

Nex, he try t'rupture my ear. He say—real loud—he say, POOR! He say that so godam loud, phone bout pop outta my hand. Then he start tellin me *I* ain poor, *he* is poor, an we is gonna make us a *deal*.

This mothahless worl' gittin nuttier an nuttier.

He say, How kin you say yer poor, you got part-min like you got, an my one hunner sides that!

I say, But Baby course I got *yer* one hunner. What the hell you think? You got some o'me an I got some o'you. How come yer so dee-diddly-godam high bout that?

He say, I *need* that one hunner.

He need it. Kee-ryess!

I bout ready t'start in yellin an never stop, but I hang on some more. I do me some considerin, best I kin unner the circumstances.

I say, Baby you want that hunner?

He say, Yeah tha's jes what he want.

I say, Okay. I say, You bring Madam car back an park him right where I unpark him from, an then you come on up t'my place an we do us some talkin.

He say, No talkin! He say, Deal is, he brings the car, he gits his hunner.

I don' know what this Whiteboy gonna say nex, he so far gone t'the moon he ain never gonna come back maybe, so all I kin do fer now is say, Okay Baby, you git the car back here an you gits yer one hunner.

Then he cool down some an he say, Kitten I thought when I come up t'yer place it weren' gonna be fer money.

Gee-zuz! Yeah! He say that!

Right now, I godam near fall thru the fuggin floor! I is all set t'let that dum mothah have wha's on my mind, but I hang on oncet agen.

I consider askin him how he think I is sposed t'keep my blackass outta jail, it don' cost him. Sep, he so dum, I fraid I lose him, I say that. Bout the time I open my big mouff, he gonna git him one more, one more dee-diddly-dum-diddly-dum idea, an he gonna flip so far out, I ain never gonna find him.

I say, real soff, I say, You think that, Sugar?

He say, Yeah he think that. An then he wanna know, Don' I *believe* bout him bein a burgler?

An I say, real soff, I say, No Lover, I don' believe that. I on'y jes think you say that counta you wanna come up my place.

He say, Crissmiss crissmiss crissmiss!

I say, Sweetheart we jes on'y had us a lil ol mis-unnerstanin.

He say, Yeah we sure done *that*!

I say, Yeah a whole wingdingin one hunner dollah misunnerstanin.

He say, Yeah! One hunner dollah worff. He say, Here I think alla time you like me, Kitten, an tha's how come you give me yer key.

I say, But Baby I do like you. Yeah! I say, I was all set t'do give an git wiff you, Honey, till you turn me roun somethin *awful*!

He say, Whaaa? Wha's this give an git?

I say, Tha's invessment, Sugar. You was gonna be my invessment. I was gonna give you fun, jes all the nice funnin you kin handle anytime you feel like it, an you was gonna make my givin worff my time.

He say—like he don' dig nothin—he say, But you give me yer *key*!

I say, Course I give you my key. How the hell you spose t'git in, you ain got no key?

He say, Invessment.

I say, Yeah Sugar, tha's it.

An he laugh. He say, Crissmiss! An he say, Alla time you want my *money*! All you want is money!

I say, Kee-ryess Jimmy, course I want money. You think I want crabs?

An then we bout t'start all over bout that all hung up hunner, cause he wanna know, Then how come I *take* his money?

Take! Ooh-wee!

I say, soff an nice, I say, But Baby, invessment spose t'come on slow an easy. First you come, I ain sure you is gonna be my invessment, so I gotta figure you fer a weekend trick till we gits goin invessment-fine, an then I gives, an you gives, an like that. Then I say, But Baby le's not talk bout that now. I say, Honeydripper you come on back t'Kitten an we sit us down an—

An he say, I git my hunner back.

I say, Oh *yeah*! Yeah yeah yeah! You git yer, *yer* hunner back. Oh yeah! I say, First you gotta come up here so's I kin give it to you.

Then he say, Okay he's on his way.

An we hang up.

Ooh-ooh-ooh-wee!

I git right back on that phone an I call up Jackie. I say Jackie that mothahless burgler turn int'policeman. He jes call up an he leave me so far out in mothahmoon land, I jes can' even see straight.

She say, Where's he at?

I say, He say he is at some Frae House some place wiff Madam car.

She say, Whaaa? Madam car?

An I jes don' say nothin.

An then she say, I'll be right over.

An we hang up.

Then, nex minit, here goes Jackie scootin in. I tell
her he's comin back wiff Madam car, but he wanna
git his hunner or he is gonna keep that big ol Kryessler Peereal.

She say, Criss! Extorshun!

I say, Yeah, jes like the law.

Madam alla time sayin how them bulls extorshun
her. An here I gotta go an git me a godam all-alone
extorshun all my very own.

But Jackie, she git t'considerin. She walkin back
an forff on my rug, considerin. Tha's okay, sep she
got her shoes on.

I say, Jackie fore you do you more considerin, how
bout takin them shoes off.

She say, Sorry. An she take 'em off. Then she go
back t'walkin an considerin agen.

I say, Maybe we gotta call in Bennie.

She say, No we ain gotta call in Bennie. No. She
say, Anybody find out he swipe that Kryessler Peereal, yer ass's gonna be *out*! She say, How come you
don' hide that car key better?

I say, I give him that car key, Jackie.

An I hol' my breath.

Jackie, she bout squat! I knowed she gonna do
jes that, I tell her how he git that car key. She grab
her head wiff her hands an she go, like, *Auh-ahugh*!
Real loud! She look like she gonna flip. She shake
real hard an plop down on my divan.

Then she take a big breath, an look better. An I
take me nother big breath too.

She say, Wha's this mothah's name?

I say, Jimmy.

She say, Criss!

She alla time sayin criss.

She say, Jimmy *WHAT*.

I say, Jes Jimmy is all I know.

An she look sick.

Then she say, You know where this house at? This place he is?

I say, No. He jes say Frae House, an I don' know what the fug is that.

She say, Fr-tit House.

I say, Oh. Fr-*tit*.

She say, No. Fr-*at*-tit House.

I say, Okay, Fr-*at*-tit House.

She say, Phew!

Then she go back t'her considerin agen.

She say, We kin do this two ways. We kin bush-wack this bull or we kin behave perfeshinal. She say, We bushwack him, he maybe stir the fuz.

Kee-ryess!

I say, How this mothah gonna raise fuz? I say, Way he doin, he can' do *that*.

She say, That Whiteboy kin call police any time he dam well wanna. She say, He kin tell 'em you *take* his money an we git our ass in jail.

I say, Gee-zuz! How come he kin do that?

She say, The law.

I say, Ooh-wee! Seem like I ain never gonna dig how this law thing work.

Jackie, she jes look sorta nasty.

Then I say, No wonner he like t' watch tee vee. All them boom boomin six-legged horse's asses cow-boy lawmen.

An she laugh. She say, Anyhow perfeshinal way is better.

I say, How that way go?

She say, He come up, we gonna be here, we give him his hunner, then we gits it back.

I say, Gee-zuz! I say, I already git me that godam hunner. Now I gotta start in all over an git it back all the hell over agen?

She say, Yeah! Tha's jes what I gotta do. Sep, this time, boff of us cats gonna haul his ashes, an we is gonna haul 'em so far off he ain never gonna find 'em agen.

Soun good. I don' know what the hell she talkin bout, but soun good, way she talk it.

She say, Fore we do anythin, we gotta git that car key.

I say, Yeah! We gotta do that.

She say, like, she snap her fingers an she say, I gotta plan. An, right now, she up an off back t'her partmin.

Nex, she right back an carryin this here lil box. Then she say, Now Kitten, start tellin me everythin you know bout this Jimmy burgler, like wha's he like and wha's he don' like.

Rest assured I came prepared for trickery. (Though not for the filthy, low, vile form of trickery I was met by.) I brought my trusty .32 Colt Special; it fits nicely into the inside pocket of my suitjacket. I figured if things got rough, I'd just draw and point it and that would be enough. I mean, I certainly didn't want to shoot anyone. Good grief! Think of the scandal!

Which (scandal) I was able to avoid. *That*, at least. As it turned out, I merely drew.

But I'm ahead of myself. Prior to this arrival, I had contacted my quarry by telephone and—after the expected resistance—clinched the deal. Which was a relief to my sleepless and jangled nerves. Nevertheless, for gosh sakes, I was about to take no chances. I was not going to underestimate her, is what I mean. Hence, the gun. And caution with a capital C.

So when I reached her apartment door, I hesitated. I took a deep breath, hitched up my belt, sucked in my stomach, threw out my chest, held back my shoulders and pinched my buttocks, assuming a military posture of preparedness. And, by gosh, I was prepared too. For darn near anything. (Anything but

177

the underhanded, subversive sort of criminality I encountered.)

I rang her doorbell and the response was surprising.
Two female voices, animated and in unison, sang
out, 'Come in.' Very musical and gay, but *two*!

And, upon opening the door, I found, there in the
middle of the floor, two colored girls (nude) (both of
them) (without a stitch on) (reminding me for all the
world of two real live characters straight out of a
Mickey Spillane mystery) (except for their color, of
course). I mean, there was Kitten, a pure chocolate
color, and this other doll, a milk-chocolate color. And
I mean she was a doll. (She later went through a
couple of very subtle and enticing movements, which
I don't think I'll be able to describe, in keeping with
my high literary plain.)

Except to say, Wow!

Anyway, I was all business, of course. And practically *knew* that the two of them being there (nude)
was no accident. I mean, I smelled trouble; I suspected tricks. And I was, as previously mentioned
above, prepared!

(Their nudity, I might add, certainly didn't excite
or distract me. I thought : JC my friend, this is no
time for romance.) (Or for functional anthropology
either, for that matter.)

I thought : On guard, JC! Lo, the sirens doth
scheme. (And I was absolutely right, too.) (Oh how
right I was!)

Quietly, but with the strength of resolve, I said,
'Kitten, I've come for my money. Here's the car key;
where's my money?'

And waited, expecting the worst. I mean, for a

moment, she didn't make a move. Neither of them did. They just sat there, smiling, looking me over, smiling.

Then—and this is the surprise which, upon review threw me—Kitten reached her hand behind herself and pulled out my money!

Just like that! Just reached behind, and there it was!

Well, she held it up to me, but I was plenty leery. I wasn't about to go near those two and let them grab me, or something. I said, 'Toss it out in front of you.'

She did.

Then I took out the gun. I mean, the ease with which she gave up the money was too much. After all the wild banshee yells and jumping about she'd done to steal it, (not to mention that knife dance she did), I never expected her to simply hand it to me with a smile on her face, for gosh sakes!

But she did. She obeyed. And I, with the gun on them, watching them both closely, inched forward stealthily and grabbed my money.

Then the other one spoke. She said, 'Hey Honey, mind closing the door? It causes a draft, you know. And besides, somebody might peek.'

I was flabbergasted! I mean, not only that she had spoken in such a casual manner, but that she had such good diction. I mean *good* for a Negro prostitute. I suspected she, unlike Kitten, was not completely illiterate.

But I was not about to let my curiosity run away with me. No!

I said, 'I'll close the door, all right. I'll close it on my way out of here.' And with these words of finality went backing towards the door—the gun still trained on them, of course.

Then, like she was rolling out of bed on a lazy Sunday morning, this other one (whose name, as it turned out, was Jackie) (though, of course, like the others, she certainly must have assumed that name; it wasn't really legally hers, no doubt)—she just sort of uncoiled slowly and rose. I mean she stood up, right in the face of my Roscoe! And, as she did so, she said. 'Hey Handsome, you forgot something.' Singsongy, like, if you get what I mean, ha ha.

Well, despite her friendly tone, I was alert. I cocked the hammer of that .32 quietly and just as nonchalant as you please. And I said, 'What have I forgotten?'

And she, in a very sexy whisper, for crying out loud, said, 'The car key.'

Which, as a matter of hard cold fact, was the exact case.

But, I mean, the way she went about informing me of my oversight—*that* was the thing. I mean, she was so casual and acted so, well, *sensuous*, if you please.

After all, a bargain's a bargain, and if one party to a bargain forgets, momentarily, to uphold his end, the other party has every right to be *other* than *sensuous*, for gosh sakes! Doesn't he?

But she wasn't concerned. Or so it seemed. It seemed like she didn't really give a darn about any key, like she was just as happy as I was that I had gotten my money back, and was more or less only stopping me for the key in order to show off her shape. (Which I won't go into.)

Anyway, I said I was sorry, it was only an over-sight, I didn't mean to walk off with the car key, that I'm not a thief, for gosh sakes, and that I had it right here in my pocket all along. Which was factual, actually.

So, still holding them at bay with the gun, I fished out the car key and tossed it on the floor in front of Jackie, who didn't even look at it, for gosh sakes. No, she just came toward me, like I was Mike Hammer, or something. But I'm not Mike Hammer, and so (I'll admit it) I became a bit rattled. I said, 'Halt! Stop right where you are! Don't take another step!'

And she did. She halted. Then, in this sickly sweet voice, she said, 'But Jimmy!' (Kitten, no doubt, had told her my name.) (That is, the name I gave Kitten —not legally mine, as referred to earlier.) 'Jimmy,' she said, 'you've got your money, and we've got our key. *Now* what's the trouble?'

'No trouble, no trouble,' I hastily assured her.

'Then simmer down, Baby,' said she.

But, I mean, the whole thing was getting too too much like some wild murder mystery.

I was on the verge of executing an abrupt about-face and taking off out the door and down the hall at a gallop when, just as cool as you please, defying the murderous weapon I held in my hand, she saun-tered up to me with this concerned expression on her face and motioned with her forefinger that she wanted to whisper in my ear.

I froze! (I mean I wasn't really frightened. I was becoming *less* rattled, even, as a matter of hard cold fact. What could she do? The game was over now; I had my money, they had their key to the Madman's car.) I thought : Obviously, JC my friend, she is un-armed. What harm can it do?

So I bent down to listen.

And, as I did so, Kitten got up and took off at a slow walk for the kitchen, glancing back at me over her shoulder, smiling that stupid smile of hers.

Well, Jackie whispered, 'The way Kitten talks, I'm missing something.'

I chuckled.

She continued. 'I'd like to find out.'

(Well, anyway, that's the *gist* of what she said.)

I tried to pretend I didn't quite get what she was driving at, but she just smiled and winked, and then pulled my head down so she could whisper again. 'Apartment 622,' said she.

I laughed and said, 'Oh no. No more, thank you.'

And she said, 'Shhh! Not so loud.' And glanced toward the kitchen. Then she whispered, 'Take your money home now, and come back later. Tonight. And, for goodness sakes, don't bring any money up to my place. I might be tempted.'

Then she shrugged her shoulders, expressively, sort of. I mean she hunched—still acting real coy and all smiles, of course.

Well, the whole bit impressed yours truly as un-believeable. I mean, she just didn't seem sincere. She seemed like Kitten when I first encountered her at the ill repute house—insincere and full of false endear-ments. But, I must admit, I was somewhat fascinated with the idea she had (indirectly and discreetly, ha ha) proposed.

I told her I'd think about it and turned to go, but she held me by the arm—the gun arm. I mean, she held me gently; she didn't grab or act like she was trying to disarm me. So I didn't fight it.

She said, and this time out loud, 'Say, Jimmy, my name's Jackie. And now that the incident of the one hundred dollars is closed, why don't you stay and have coffee with us?'

Before I could answer, she called to Kitten : 'Is that okay with you, Sweetie?'

And Kitten poked her head out of the kitchen and said, yes, it was okay with her, that she'd fix three cups.

Then Jackie sort of guided me to the couch, all the time talking—very casually—about how there's nothing like a good cup of coffee to make a person feel better, especially in the morning. And I agreed. (How could I ever have suspected the depths to which these women would stoop?) I wasn't dropping my guard, but I put the gun in my pocket and went along with her. I thought : What the heck, James Cartwright Holland, obviously you have the upper hand now. (This, as it turned out, wasn't entirely accurate.) These girls are only being friendly now. (The sneaks!) There's no reason why you can't pause for a moment; as long as they're being such good sports.

Which, as it turned out, they weren't. No, not at all!

So, right off the bat, the next thing I know, there I am sitting on the couch sipping coffee with these two ladies of ill repute. The coffee table was between us. *That*, thought old JC, is as it should be. I was on the couch and they were on the floor, on the other side of the coffee table. We were having a friendly little discussion, Jackie and I, about—first, Kitten's blatant destruction of the TV set, which even now lay right where she'd left it, and second, about the space race. I was feeling a little sorry for Kitten; I mean, Jackie and I were doing all the talking and Kitten was left completely out of our conversation, especially when we got deep into the space race. Poor Kitten, thought I—just sitting there, staring into her cup.

But this Jackie, she was pretty impressive! (I mean, as I thought at the time, having since revised my thinking radically.)

Now, please, Dear Reader, get this picture: Me (dressed and packing my trusty .32) (wearing the same suit I had been wearing, off and on, since the night before) (but with a change of underwear and with a clean white shirt and also with my valuable papers and wallet in my pocket) and these two women (colored and undressed) on the far side of the coffee table. Talk—interesting and verging on the intellectual side between Jackie and I, with Kitten silent and a bit sad. (Understandably, I thought.)

Apparently!

Then— Holy Christmas!

That quick! It happened that quick! I mean one minute I was okay, the next I wasn't even *there*!

And this time when I say Bamb, I mean B-A-M-B, Bamb!

Lights out!

The next thing I became aware of was motion. Yes, motion. My motion. I was being half-dragged, half-walked down this hallway (gradually discovering, as I went, that it was the apartment house hallway) by some guy (whom, I also gradually discovered, was the same beady-eyed character who had directed me to the ill repute house in the first place) and then we got on the elevator and I went back to sleep. I mean I sort of dozed off in the elevator, only to be jolted awake again and find this character guiding me across that big rug through the lobby and to the front door.

Upon taking some deep breaths of fresh air, my brain recovered to function well enough for me to realize they had slipped me something in that coffee. That much I realized at that moment.

The next thing I knew, however, there was this crowd of colored people standing in sort of a semi-circle, looking at me and laughing. I mean, in my drugged state, about all I could see were these Negroid faces and teeth, and all I could hear was laughter. I was too far gone even to be concerned about what they were laughing at.

Which, I soon discovered, was my attire. Because the next instant—or so it seemed—I was alone in the back of this taxi. I was, to be exact, prone on the backseat. I managed to pull myself up and look around and discover that I was in a taxi.

And also to see how I was dressed. (Or not dressed.) That is : No underwear ! No socks ! No shirt and tie ! Just my shoes (untied) and my suit (turned inside out.)

I mean, there I was, the victim of two ill repute women who had stooped to using drugs in the lowest possible sort of doublecross, then to add insult to injury, had stripped me of my clothes—all but the suit, turned inside out !

Well, I slumped. I mean, I couldn't help slumping —being drugged and practically undressed, and finding sleep, or a half-sickening state of unconsciousness, irresistible. I slumped and slept and woke up in front of the frat house, with the cab driver hovering over me, demanding, of all things, money!

Money, for gosh sakes!

Well, I tried to search my pockets but, being turned inside out and in my present sleep-bound state, was unable to ascertain much of anything from that search, except that they had also stolen my .32. So I told the driver he'd have to wait a while so I could go into the frat house and get some money.

Fortunately, however, he elected to help me into the house instead of waiting. *Fortunately*, because I don't think I could have made it alone. Well, he helped me up to the second floor and into my room, collecting this howling mob of brothers as we went. They of course, thought it was funny and wanted to know what happened.

I, of course, didn't see much humor in the situation—especially at that time—and was in no mood for conversation.

I slept. When I got to my room, I just flopped on my bed and slept.

And when I came to, found myself still dressed in my suit turned inside out, with Hank leaning over me with this leer of his, telling me I owed him money for my taxi fare.

I ignored him. I also ignored all the brothers who came flooding in, asking what happened. Though, as I recuperated, I was able to see how—without knowing the sordid, criminal details—a person might be amused by the way I looked. (They found especially funny the fact that my university identification card had been pinned to the back of my inside-out coat, and just beneath the card, on a separate and large piece of paper, in pencil, someone had written, *Please Deliver*.)

The brothers have since asked many questions and also tried to speculate for themselves on the general question : How did J. C. Holland get himself into such a mess, and what, exactly, was the nature of the mess he got himself into?

I have turned a deaf ear to such questions and ignored such of their speculations which various jerks have voiced. They have continued to speculate and I have continued to remain silent on the subject.

For one thing, I'm not sure I could answer to their satisfaction. For another, I'm hard at work boning up on biology, psychology, French. (And glad to report that I'm improving, too. Yes, my grades definitely show a marked improvement this half semester.) (I mean, if that fantastic and financially tragic weekend did nothing else for me—which it did—it did teach me a valuable lesson : to wit : I now realize what my scholastic trouble was—I did not follow instructions. I mean, not as *well* as I should have. That's the secret, and by discovering it I have at last finally made the complete adjustment to higher education. I now pay strict attention and follow instructions to the letter, and am getting along very well.) (I don't mean to boast, but I *am*.)

And . . . Well, that's about all there is to tell. Though, just to round it out, I might add I had a terrible time of it, trying to cover up my financial embarrassment during that period of complete and utter destitution until my next check arrived. During which Barbara felt somehow compelled to increase the injury and embarrassment by paying both our ways to the Playhouse so we wouldn't have to cancel our date. (Not only that, but she, too, has heard about my inside-out attire when I returned that Sunday, and has, in her own curious way, tried to find out what happened.) (By *curious* way, I mean she has been strangely attentive recently—a development in our relationship which is causing me concern.)

Also, I've thought of going back to Kitten's place for another attempt to reclaim my stolen money, but the awful financial (as well as personal) embarrassment that weekend recalls gives rise to thoughtful hesitation.

Jackie's invessment, he's a teecher at the college. He come t'see Jackie, she bring him down my place, an we tell him how we do Jimmy.

He laugh, say it serve Jimmy right.

I don' like the way we gotta do Jimmy. I don' laugh.

Way we do, we git couple-a Jackie's pills an put 'em in coffee an git Jimmy t'drink the coffee. Then he jes pop off t'sleep. We takes his money, an this piece he come packin, an I git my partmin key, an then we put him in his clothes ass backwar's, an pin a label on him, an then we gits Bennie t'carry him down an put him in a cab.

Jackie say, We fix him so he don' wanna pull that trick agen.

An I spect we do.

I say, Jackie I don' like bein so mean, even t'some dum Jimmy the burgler.

She say, Kitten we gotta be mean, we ain got no choice.

Jackie's invessment, he say, Yeah tha's how the worl' is, you gotta be mean, else you gonna git peed on.

Still, don' seem right. Like, Jackie an her invessment, they give an git real fine. He bring her all kinda presents, an he alla time hide money roun her partmin. They laugh an dance an play turnabout.

She-it! Make me feel real sad. On'y Jimmy was better at considerin an not so godam mean, me an him coulda had us a nice time. I can' help wonnerin, maybe I done somethin wrong. Maybe I coulda fix it up so's we unnerstan each others better an don' git all hung up on that mothahhumpin hunner.

Anyhow, Jackie's loverman, he been tellin me bout this here college way far away, they teech readin. Yeah! He say, They kin teech readin by showin movies, like.

Ooh-wee!

I say, Spose some blackass Pickaninny cat like me wanna learn readin?

He say, You kin go t'this college.

An then he wanna know, What is I considerin doin, oncet I kin read real good?

I tell him. I say—right in front o' Jackie—I say, I wanna find out how come nobody kin truss nobody in this mothahflippin muddlefuggin worl', how come everybody gotta ack mean. I wanna know how come my blackass can' ack nice an give an git, give an git, like him an Jackie do. How come I alla time gotta git an git, like a mothahless burgler.

Nex, him an Jackie, they boff start in jawin at oncet. Then Jackie cork ass an let her Whiteboy loverman talk, an he say, Tha's a good queshun, Kitten. He say, All kinda folks been tryin t'find out a how come fer that queshun fer hunners an hunners o'years.

Jackie say, Kitten we been all over that an I tol' you you gotta *know* yer gonna git fore you start givin.

But that don' seem right neither. How is I gonna find out I is gonna git, I don' do no givin first?

What a muddlefuggin mix up! Gee-zuz!

Jackie's invessment, he think so too. He say he wanna see me readin so's I kin hunt me up some ansers.

An that soun pritty good, sep nex, I go an ask him which books got the ansers, an he say well they ain none got no final ansers.

Then how the hell m'I spose t'find ansers them books don' got.

He gone, Jackie say, Soon's they close the cat-house fer local leckshuns, her an Madam gonna send me way far away t'this mothahless readin college, an I is gonna come back jes a-readin my blackass t'the moon an back!

I say, No-oh-oh! No fuggin readin college fer me! I say, I can' find me no ansers in them big fatass books, I don' care t'do no readin. Sides, I git t'readin, I fraid I is gonna flip my lid. Yeah! I say, Jackie steada readin, what I wanna learn, I wanna learn pills! Like, you git some dum Jimmy-style Whiteboy an you can' unnerstan him an he can' unnerstan you, pills is how you do him. Yeah! Pills best!

Jackie say, She kin teech me pills okay, an I kin learn readin too.

I say, No readin fer me. No! I say, I ain goin all by myseff t'no way far away college, cause them Jimmy-style Whiteboys'd scare my blackass blue!

She consider what I tell her, an she an Madam talk, an then Jackie tell me she gonna make me a bargain. She say, We go t'gether. Yeah! She say, She wanna do her some more learnin too, so me an her kin go t'gether.

I been considerin her bargain. I been considerin maybe I take me a blade, I kin git back okay. Fack, maybe what I oughtta do, I oughtta take me my great big cottinpickin Pickaninny grin an a whole lotta pills. Steada some ol blade.

Yeah! Wiff pills, I don' need no blade.

I take me my grin an my pills case some mothahless Whiteboy College Joe try him some fancy gittin an gittin on my poor ol blackass Pickaninny me, maybe I kin go an git back, an then do me some oohwee big fatass book readin, an maybe find out jes what the tee vee terrible trouble wiff them mothahjumpin boom boomin Whitefolks, they can' give an git, an gotta ack mean alla time.

Anyhow, I spect me an Jackie is gonna go. My one hunner an that other loot I got from Jimmy, she put that wiff Bennie in my bank count. She say tha's fer me t'go readin college on.

So come local leckshun time an the cathouse shut down fer awhile, I spect we is gonna go. Meantime, Jackie is teechin me pills.